First published in 2013 as *Frühling der Barbaren* by Jonas Lüscher
Copyright © Verlag CH Beck oHG, Munich 2013

First published in Great Britain by Haus Publishing in 2014
Haus Publishing
70 Cadogan Place,
London SW1X 9AH
www.hauspublishing.com

'The Axe Handles', Gary Snyder, 1983, in *Axe Handles: Poems* by Gary Snyder,
Counterpoint Press, San Francisco, reprinted by kind permission of
Counterpoint Press.

English translation copyright © Peter Lewis, 2014

Peter Lewis dedicates this translation to his
fellow translator and friend Tom Morrison (1960–2014).

The rights of the author have been asserted.

Print ISBN: 978-1-908323-83-5
Ebook ISBN: 978-1-908323-84-2

Typeset in Garamond by MacGuru Ltd
info@macguru.org.uk

Printed and bound in the UK by TJ International

This book has been translated with the support of the Swiss Arts Council
Pro Helvetia

swiss arts council
pr☐helvetia

BARBARIAN SPRING

by
JONAS LÜSCHER

translated by
PETER LEWIS

What is 'barbarism' in actual fact? It is not the same thing as cultural primitivism, a turning-back of the clock. [...] It is a state in which many of the values of an advanced civilisation are present, but without that social and moral coherence which is the prerequisite for a culture to function rationally. But it is precisely for this reason that 'barbarism' is also a creative process: once the overall coherence of a culture is shattered, the path lies open for a renewal of creativity. Yet there is no denying that this path may lead through a total collapse of political and economic life, and through centuries of spiritual and material impoverishment and dreadful suffering. Our own particular stamp of civilisation and culture may not survive unbroken, but we may be certain that the fruits of civilisation and culture will survive in some form. There is no historical basis for believing that the end result will be some 'tabula rasa'.

Franz Borkenau

1

'NO,' SAID PREISING, 'you're asking the wrong questions', and as if to emphasise his objection he suddenly stopped dead on the gravel path. This habit of his annoyed me, as it made our strolls feel like the wheezy perambulations of old, overweight Basset hounds. And yet I continued to take a daily constitutional with Preising for, despite his many irritating quirks, in this place he was still the person whose company I most enjoyed. 'No', he repeated, finally moving off again, 'you're asking the wrong questions.'

For all Preising's loquaciousness, he set great store by what he said, and always knew precisely what questions he wanted people to ask him – ones which ensured that the torrent of words flowing from him would take the course he intended. And so I, who to all intents and purposes was a prisoner here, had little choice but to go along with him.

'Look here,' he said, 'I'll prove it to you. À propos of which, I'll tell you a little story.' *À propos*, for heaven's sake! – that was another one of his affectations, larding his speech with archaic turns of phrase he knew full well nobody else used anymore. Even so, it was a foible which I fear had begun to rub off on me over the course of the last few weeks. Sometimes I seriously doubted whether we were good for one another, Preising and me.

'A story,' he promised, 'with a moral to it. A tale full

of incredible twists and turns, nail-biting adventures and exotic temptations.'

If you're expecting some sleazy story at this juncture, you couldn't be more wrong. Preising never spoke about his sex life. I knew him well enough not to fear that. In fact, I could only conjecture whether he even had a sex life. It was certainly hard to imagine. Then again, appearances can be deceptive. After all, when I look at myself in the mirror, I sometimes wonder how a lifeless person like me had managed one.

Before launching into his story, Preising interrupted our walk again and stood staring at the horizon – which in our case was very close, namely the top of the high yellow perimeter wall – as if gazing back into the past. He narrowed his eyes, sniffed and pursed his narrow lips. 'Maybe,' he finally began, 'none of this would ever have happened if Prodanovic hadn't sent me on holiday.'

Though he was ultimately responsible for Preising's admission to this place, Prodanovic wasn't his doctor. No, Prodanovic was that young – actually not so young any more now, but still brilliant – employee of Preising's whose invention of the Wolfram CBC circuit, which every mobile phone mast in the world needed in order to function, had saved the television aerial concern Preising had inherited from impending bankruptcy, propelling it to the dizzy heights of global market leader in CBC circuitry.

Preising's father, who put off dying just long enough for his son to complete the Business Studies degree he'd interrupted by spending eighteen months at a private

Parisian singing school, bequeathed Preising his TV-aerial factory with 35 employees at a time when cable television had already gained a firm foothold. The turnover of the company, which had grown from his grandfather's original inductor and potentiometer manufacturing business, where Preising's forbears had worn their fingers to the bone twisting thin copper wires, was at that juncture almost entirely accounted for by the production of metre-long aerials for radio hams to install on their roofs – competitively priced thanks to their almost total lack of branching – but unfortunately, radio hams were a dying breed, too.

So it was that Preising, through no fault of his own, found himself at the helm of a failing company that was badly in need of a shake-up, and there was no question that the business would have gone under if the young instrument engineer Prodanovic hadn't developed the Wolfram CBC circuit and taken charge of the firm. Preising, then, had Prodanovic to thank for making him not only a wealthy proprietor, but also chairman of a company with a workforce of 1,500 and branches on all five continents. At least, that was how things appeared to the outside world; in reality, for a long time the day-to-day running of the dynamic enterprise, which now went by the dynamic-sounding name of *Prixxing*, had been in the hands of Prodanovic and his team of thrusting high achievers and go-getters.

Yet as the public face of the firm, Preising was still much in demand, and Prodanovic was well aware that, if Preising did serve any useful purpose, then it was to convey a sense of permanence, as the steadfast presiding spirit of a fourth-generation family firm. That was the only role that Prodanovic, the son of a Bosnian buffet waiter, didn't presume to fill himself. After all, he was the first to admit that anything to do with the Balkans positively shrieked instability – an impression to be avoided in business at all costs. Whenever his busy schedule allowed, Prodanovic liked to give talks at inner-city problem schools, presenting himself as a shining example of successful integration. It was the very same Prodanovic, equipped with full power of attorney over the company, who had packed Preising off on holiday, something he was wont to do whenever important decisions were pending.

Now, I realised straight away that, even with the first sentence of his story, Preising had effectively succeeded in absolving himself of all responsibility for the events that subsequently unfolded.

He didn't even have to decide where to go on holiday. The ever-efficient Prodanovic always endeavoured to combine pleasure with business. Which in this case meant Preising flying to Tunisia and visiting one of their suppliers, whose factory was located in a low corrugated-iron shed in one of the industrial estates on the outskirts of Sfax, on the road to Tunis. Slim Malouch, the owner of the assembly plant, was a wheeler-dealer with a wide portfolio of interests, including electronic goods, phosphates and upmarket tourism. He owned a string of exclusive hotels, and Preising would be his guest.

Malouch was keen to do business with anyone who had

anything to do with telecommunications, not only because he'd identified that that was where the future lay – he and every other entrepreneur – but also because he saw it as the only way of saving his family enterprise. Sure, he had four clever and, as Preising assured me, really very good-looking daughters but he was afraid that current circumstances in Tunisia made it impossible for him to entrust them with the running of the family's various concerns. Accordingly, this responsibility fell entirely upon the shoulders of his son. Shoulders which Foued Malouch had already burdened with the moral responsibility of a course in Ecological Geology in Paris, making it quite out of the question for him to now head up a firm that earned the lion's share of its profits from phosphates, which ended up as chemical fertiliser on the salad-growing fields of Europe. Foued even went so far as to threaten his father with the prospect of dropping out and trying his luck on an organic farm in the Lot *département*. Preising could see for himself that Slim Malouch wasn't just a respectable man, he was also prudent and so was trying to diversify from phosphates into telecommunications, and hoped to further this aim by getting to know Preising.

Preising was all set, then, to exchange the fogs of midland Switzerland for the balmy Tunisian spring. He swapped his customary tweed jacket and burgundy cords for a houndstooth jacket the colour of an egg nog and a pair of chinos with sharp creases; in all honesty, he found this ensemble ludicrous, but his housekeeper had laid it out ready for him and he was afraid of offending her by spurning it. And so, with his face set in an indulgent smile, he found himself climbing into the passenger seat of her car – he didn't own one himself – and having her drive him to the airport.

'The flight was a real pleasure,' Preising assured me. 'I even broke the habit of a lifetime and had a drink. The stewardess had misheard me and brought me a scotch instead of a fruit juice. I accepted it anyhow because I felt sorry for her, with her dumpy figure, which stood in such stark contrast to all the stylised gazelle logos on her uniform. It's true, she really wasn't a looker, and certain passengers who thought their purchase of a ticket entitled them to something more were giving her a hard time. I'd have felt bad not taking every opportunity I could to be nice to her, so I felt obliged to accept a second scotch, and then a third.'

Slim Malouch, accompanied by his eldest daughter, greeted Preising in the over-air-conditioned arrivals hall at Tunis–Carthage airport and when Preising saw, in the heat outside the building, the enviably imperious way in which Malouch shooed away the taxi drivers and beckoned to his personal chauffeur, he was fleetingly tempted to give credence to the rumour that his hosts were the illegitimate son of Roger Trinquier – author of the seminal work *Modern Warfare* – and his Algerian mistress, who had allegedly fled the country on the night the French pulled out of the Maghreb and crossed the desert into Tunisia, with the infant Slim cradled in her arms. There, her physical charms and her skills as a typist soon saw her become the secretary, and then the wife, of a backbencher from the Néo-Destour Party. Her husband was hatching a plan to assassinate President Bourguiba, and was only thwarted by a fatal heart attack during a sitting of parliament; and so, because he'd supposedly died in the service of the fatherland, he was posthumously decorated, while his wife, the former courtesan of the French torturer of Algerians, was granted a generous state pension.

Then again, Preising recalled, the source of this rumour was unreliable. He'd heard it from a man called Moncef Daghfous who, aside from being Malouch's main competitor, had also made Preising an offer to assemble the CBC circuits at a far lower unit cost in his factory on the outskirts of Tunis. He openly confessed that his ability to undercut Malouch was mainly due to the fact that he was employing underage Dinka refugees who'd fled the conflict in Darfur. Dab-handed little chaps, he called them. Preising would have been only too happy to turn the offer down flat, but the child labour thing wasn't as clear-cut as it seemed. He called to mind an evening at the neo-liberal business club Prodanovic belonged to, where the person next to him at dinner had explained what a delicate subject child labour was. Much more problematic than your average do-gooder might like to think, it really wasn't such a straightforward matter at all, and under certain circumstances it could even be the lesser of two evils. Preising was unsure if those circumstances applied to the current case, because frankly he'd had trouble following what his young dinner companion was driving at. In any event, he put off making a decision; he'd need to consult Prodanovic first, and he kept stalling Moncef Daghfous with flimsy excuses.

Daghfous had got the wrong idea about Preising. He

clearly took him to be some chancer. Having tarred his rival Slim Malouch with a shady past and pitched an unbeatably cheap price and yet still failed to strike a deal with Preising, he wheeled out the big guns and summoned his six daughters. Preising could take his pick, he said, they were all available and all of marriageable age, only the second one from the left was already spoken for, but if Preising really insisted, then he, Daghfous, would arrange for the fiancé to be involved in a car crash, though that kind of thing was really tricky to organise and besides, the other five were just as good as the one who was engaged. *Voilà*, he said, spreading out his palms and gesturing towards his daughters. *Voilà*, repeated Preising, not knowing what else to say.

Of course, Preising was shocked by this, but he was also an avowed cultural relativist of a completely unchauvinistic kind. His liberalism was a lukewarm variety of relativism. All the same, on our walks he was always ready to flaunt his ethics of virtue like some religious monstrance. Preising, the great devotee of Aristotle's Doctrine of the Mean, who was content in the knowledge that the mean wasn't some mathematical postulate, but a concept that needed to be determined afresh on a case-by-case basis. Here, though, different worlds collided. Here extreme caution was called for. And this business with Daghfous' daughters was a particularly problematic case that gave him much pause for thought.

I was afraid his story was going to degenerate into some Maghrebian *Scheherazade*, all about exotic temptations, with Preising having to choose between six underage Tunisian girls like he was selecting from the cheeseboard at the Restaurant Kronenhalle in Zurich. Perhaps his tale was about to turn sleazy after all.

'But just when things were starting to go pear-shaped,' he went on, 'and the man began reproaching me, saying that evidently I didn't find his daughters attractive enough and that maybe he should send them away and call in his three sons instead, and it was all I could do to reassure him that my problem was that I was spoilt for choice, since each of the girls was so utterly ravishing in her own way, while all the time desperately searching for a polite way to decline his offer without mortally offending him, he was suddenly interrupted by a servant whose face was flushed with alarm. It seemed that one of Daghfous' phosphate plants had gone up in flames. Daghfous hastily left me in the care of his daughters – who fussed over me in a truly touching manner – and dashed out of the room, promising to be back in a trice to find out which one I'd plumped for.'

In the event, though, it never came to that. While the daughters, under the supervision of an old chaperone, were serving tea and sweetmeats, Daghfous was attempting, with flailing arms and a volley of profane threats, to herd his workforce back into the plant to tackle the blaze. When all his gesticulations and curses fell on deaf ears, he grabbed a bucket of sand and a spade himself and, *pour encourager les autres,* strode towards the burning building, just in time to meet a shock wave coming in the opposite direction; unleashed by a massive explosion, it tore Moncef Daghfous' head from his body and distributed bits of his phosphate plant – corrugated iron, old-fashioned conveyor belts, French excavators and American wheel-loaders – across a wide radius of the surrounding rocky landscape.

'When the same servant came back to impart the tragic news, I fully expected a traditional display of grief. Loud wailing, hair-tearing, extravagant clawing at faces contorted in pain, fainting fits and all that kind of thing. But instead the six daughters just looked at one another in silence, cleared away the tea glasses and the silver pot and deposited me out on the street with a half-eaten piece of baklava in my hand.'

You could never be sure whether Preising's stories were true or not, but that wasn't the point. What mattered to him was the moral of the story. He firmly believed that every tale worth telling had one. For the most part, his stories bore witness to his own prudence, of which he was inordinately proud.

Yet Dr Betschart regarded Preising's prudence as a suitable case for treatment, a psychopathology for which she was still, three weeks after his referral to the institute, trying to find the correct clinical description. The diagnosis appeared difficult, the symptoms unclear, and the obduracy of the patient, who veered between being charming and amiable on the one hand and tiresomely stubborn on the other, wasn't exactly helping either.

My common depression was infinitely easier to diagnose

and at the same time fundamentally less interesting. Yet in our inability to see ourselves as capable of taking action we were alike, Preising and I. He managed to construe this evident failing as a virtue. I, on the other hand, am greatly bothered by it. Yet doing anything about it would mean taking action.

'In any event,' Preising continued, 'the source was unreliable, and Slim Malouch's behaviour gave me no cause whatever to doubt his unimpeachable pedigree. Courteously, he ushered me into the back seat of a French limousine – whose positively maritime handling characteristics on the potholed road to Tunis put me in mind of a camel ride... but more on camels presently,' Preising interjected, '– next to his daughter Saida before closing the door behind me and getting into the driver's seat of a 4×4, which I'd completely failed to spot had pulled up alongside us. Holding his mobile to his ear and giving us a graceful wave, he roared past us. I wouldn't see him again until that evening. He was terribly sorry, he'd told me before leaving, he was rushed off his feet that day, but Saida would look after me and take me to the hotel she managed, where I was to spend the first night of my stay.

'On the drive into town, Saida pointed out all the places of interest through the limousine's tinted windows; her gracious demeanour dispelled any lingering doubts I may have had about the Malouch family. A glimpse of the Lac de Tunis, a fleeting prospect of the Avenue Habib Bourguiba, the Magasin Général, a few picturesque doorways. I turned my head this way and that, feigning interest as though I was seeing all this for the first time. Malouch didn't need to know that, barely a year before, I'd already spent several days in Tunis at the invitation of his rival Moncef Daghfous.

'The car drew up in front of a four-storey building in a side street off the Place de la Victoire. It was whitewashed with blue-painted shutters and liberally adorned with slim pillars and crenellations in the Moorish style. "*L'Hôtel d'Elisha*", Saida announced, as the chauffeur opened the door for me. "Elisha, also known by her Roman name Dido, the founder and ruler of Carthage."'

'Ah, Dido,' Preising said, pursing his lips like a connoisseur and stopping in his tracks once more. 'Of all the deities and demigods,' he declaimed, 'Dido was always my favourite, the closest to my heart you might say. You've got to admire the way she told her subjects that it was everyone's duty to sacrifice themselves to save the Fatherland, though I'm sure you'd agree' – here he cast a glance at me – 'that Motherland would be more appropriate in the case of Carthage, or if they refused, that they'd be put to death. And when the queen's turn duly came, after having had to agree to marry that unprincipled despot Iarbas, the son of Jupiter and the Libyan nymph Garamantis, to stop him from sacking Carthage, she didn't waver for a moment but had a funeral pyre built and lit and threw herself onto it and ran herself through with a sword – there's a heart-rending illustration of it in the Vatican Virgil. You know,' he continued, placing his hand between my shoulder blades and gently propelling me forwards, as if I'd been the one who'd interrupted our walk, 'there's an object lesson for the business community there. If you're a CEO and make some mission statement, then no question about it, the buck stops with you. If photocopying costs are too high, say, and you issue a directive for people to use the copier less, then you should lead by example, and if that proves too much of an effort, then you should give up copying altogether.'

And so, whistling the opening bars of Purcell's *Dido and Aeneas* to himself, he was escorted into the *Hôtel d'Elisha* by the manageress Saida Malouch. He insisted on calling it the 'Hôtel Dido' – after all, he reasoned, that was the name by which the beloved queen was known to her subjects. The décor inside this cosmopolitan boutique establishment, which any number of glossy magazines featured under the rubric 'Hideaway', remained predominantly Moorish. The interior designers had gone for whitewashed walls and floors of dove-blue concrete, alternating with dark floorboards, where various unusual chairs had been placed. The walls were decorated with a few depictions of Dido from different eras.

Features typical of the country, or rather what the international hideaway-seeker would imagine were typical, appeared here and there as little ironic references. A fez serving as a shade for a bedside lamp, a few ornamental glazed tiles set haphazardly into the cement floor, the odd tassel here, a bit of carved wood there. And, as a recurrent motif, oxhides, a detail that Preising noted with the especial delight of someone in the know.

'Oxhides!' Even recounting it to me now, he was beside

himself with pleasure. 'Oxhides – Dido – oxhides, get it? Dido and the Oxhide, no?' he prompted. I shrugged my shoulders, uncomprehending. By now, Preising was in full flow. 'The Isoperimetric Problem, also known as Dido's Problem?'

He had an acquaintance who regularly sent him books about all the famous riddles and marvels of mathematics: Fermat's Last Theorem, Goldbach's Conjecture, The Travelling Salesman Problem. Preising read them, because he really did enjoy reading, but hated being faced with stacked shelves in bookshops and having to choose a book for himself. He also liked baffling people like me with amazing stories from the world of numbers.

People like me, though, aren't easily baffled. He should have realised that by now. Bafflement means encountering some resistance from the world around you, yet someone like me provides hardly any contact surface for it to attack, and the same was true of Preising himself. Even so, he didn't want to pass up the opportunity to regale me with the tale of Dido and the Oxhide.

'Dido and her retinue,' he lectured me, 'had quit Tyre in fear of Pygmalion's wrath, and after putting in at Cyprus kidnapped fifty women – some sources even say eighty – before fetching up on the coast of North Africa. Dido asked the people there for a tract of land for herself and her entourage, only as much, she said, as could be encompassed by a single oxhide. The beautiful refugee was readily granted her wish. But then Dido proceeded to slice the hide into the thinnest strips imaginable and, laying it out in a semi-circle, claimed the large chunk of coastline it encompassed as her own.'

The thought of such ingenuity inhabiting a beautiful woman from mythology – I got the distinct impression Preising preferred mythological women to real women – put a spring in his step, and so both our walk and his story began to pick up speed.

'I'll pass over the dinner at Malouch's house,' Preising said. 'Exquisite, elegant, exotic. And his wife – *très charmante*, but surprisingly modern. The house, a palace, was quite traditional, only with lots of televisions. All in all, a very nice occasion, but still a business dinner. Not that we discussed much business. But I'll skip telling you about that, it doesn't really have any bearing on the main story. Nor does my visit to the souk the next morning with Saida. Truly overwhelming. The smells. But that's another story. Oh, and the colours as well, quite breathtaking.

'So, anyway, around midday I left Tunis in a 4×4, with one of Slim Malouch's employees at the wheel. Saida was sitting in the back with me, and her assistant was in the front passenger's seat. We soon left the outer suburbs of the city behind us, and I began to enjoy our journey through the ever more barren landscape. Our destination was the Tschub Oasis, where Saida ran another of her father's luxury hotels. As we drove along, she discussed with her assistant the precarious state of the British financial system. Over the past few days, the pound had plummeted in value. They were very concerned that the flow of English guests might dry up. And it was true, at that time the situation was confused and deeply troubling. New scandals were coming to light on an almost daily basis. The entanglements among the English banks, and between the banks and other institutions faced with ruin, grew ever more opaque. Saida and her colleague, who both spoke very professionally about the crisis and seemed well informed, feared the worst. For my part, I'd resolved a few days before to pay no more attention to the whole mess. I'd made it a principle of mine to leave anything beyond my sphere of competence and knowledge off my list of things to worry about, a rule which I've found has served me well thus far.

'I think the desert must be the sort of landscape I relate to the most. Its emptiness, its vastness and the dead-straight road we were bowling along. As soon as we'd left the hilly hinterland behind us and the first outlying dunes of the massive sea of sand came into view, I too left everything behind me – the city's noise, Slim Malouch's relentless flattery and Prodanovic's constant look of worry.

'The dead camels wrenched me abruptly from my dreamy contemplation of the passing dunes. In fact, the scene that met our eyes not thirty metres in front of us seemed to render us all speechless for a moment, and caused our driver to brake sharply and bring the car to a halt. A silver monster of a tour bus, with wing mirrors sticking out into the road like elephant's ears, stood motionless in front of us on the dark asphalt strip, reflecting the desert sun. All around it lay ten or so – maybe as many as fifteen – camels, some of them on their own and some in tangled heaps of bony limbs and flaccid humps. Their twisted necks lying lifelessly on the road presented a obscene spectacle. One of the animals had literally wrapped itself around the closely spaced twin front axles of the bus. Its neck, unnaturally stretched, hung limply over the hot rubber of the massive tyre, its tongue lolled out of its mouth between its bared yellow teeth and one of its legs, wedged between the wheel and the body-work, was pointing skywards, with the calloused foot bent at an acute angle. Trapped between the two wheels, the camel's body had been unable to withstand the pressure, and its intestines were spilling out all over the road.

'A small crowd had gathered round the lifeless bodies. The atmosphere was charged, to say the least. A couple of soldiers in camouflage and green berets were trying to placate five or six furious Bedouin, some of whom were also armed. Behind the soldiers, sweating profusely and with a nasty gash on his forehead, stood the coach driver, in a pale blue short-sleeved shirt, loudly berating the camel drivers. The faces of several tourists loomed up dimly behind the mirrored windows of the bus, some ashen as they gawped at the scene, while others were pressing their noses to the glass and trying to capture as much as they could on their memory cards so they could illustrate their account with pictures when they told their friends back home.'

In the meantime, our stroll had taken us to the perimeter, where we turned left onto a broad gravel path running the length of the yellow wall. Preising was really quite animated by this stage. He was gesticulating extravagantly and every now and then would throw in a little skipping step, or even two or three. 'Saida gave vent to two exple-tives,' he continued, 'which I'd never have imagined were in her vocabulary. One in English, the other in French. Literally translated, they both expressed the same basic idea. She stepped out of the car, and her assistant and I did likewise.'

Preising and his companions stood there, behind the open doors of the 4×4. A searing heat beat down on their heads. Above the dead camels and the hot tarmac, the air was shimmering with a viscosity so dense you could almost see the sound waves. The heat haze was a flickering visualisation of the raised voices and the gut-wrenching bellowing of a dying camel. Saida asked him to wait by the car and then, with her assistant at her side, set off purposefully towards the scene of carnage. Suddenly, the cacophonous argument was cut short by the crack of a single gunshot. Preising saw how Saida was pulled to the ground by her colleague and, slamming the doors behind him, took cover by throwing himself as fast as he could down onto the cool leather of the back seat. He could faintly make out the shrieks of alarm coming from within the coach and the loud shouts of the soldiers. Only the roaring of the dying camel had fallen silent. All guns were trained on a man who, behind the other's backs, had delivered the *coup de grâce* to the camel with a shot from his carbine right between the animal's wide-open eyes.

Saida quickly got to her feet, brushed the dust off her elegant trouser-suit and weighed in to the argument. Preising remained in the car, following events from a safe distance. Saida soon got the situation under control. Preising was able to see at first hand how, both here in the desert and on the streets of Tunis, she exuded boundless self-confidence and an innate air of authority.

'It was loud, it was hectic and pretty aggressive, too,' Preising recounted with obvious disapproval. 'And it went on and on, without the slightest hint of a resolution. In these parts of the world arguments carry quite a different weight and follow a totally different set of rules. Never, ever, try to get involved; you're on a hiding to nothing, I promise you. You'll always end up saying the wrong thing. I'd even go so far as to say that it's a sport for them. Argument for argument's sake. And on no account should you ever tell them to calm down and settle the matter peaceably. For them, getting agitated is the whole point.' He cast me a look of grave concern before continuing: 'As for me, I soon get fed up with this kind of set-to. They almost invariably go nowhere. So I asked our driver to pass me over the *Financial Times*, which was lying on the dashboard.

'The newspaper was running only one story, it seemed – the alarming re-emergence of the financial crisis, and above all the precarious position Britain now found herself in, thanks to the collapse of the Royal Bank of Scotland, which the government had had a more than 80 percent stake in since the banking crash of 2008. In the space of just 24 hours, RBS's predicament had triggered national – no, global – chaos, because in its wake, Lloyds Banking Group, over 70 percent state-owned, had also folded, but unbeknownst to the government, these institutions had become so heavily involved in lending junk sub-prime mortgages in Bangalore and Malaya that analysts from all the leading newspapers were expressing grave doubts whether Her Majesty's Government would ever be able to guarantee people's savings. In turn, such stories sparked an unprecedented run on banks throughout the United Kingdom. The newspaper I was reading had a photograph of events at a branch in the small town of Ilfracombe in Devon, which I know well from having spent a cycling holiday there in my youth and which I remembered as a thoroughly sleepy place, but in comparison to the scene caught in the picture, what was happening on the other side of the 4×4's broad windscreen, with the furious row still raging and the dead camels, seemed an image of positive peace and harmony. When their savings are at stake, people become animals.'

Out there in the desert, the gunman was now putting on quite a moving performance. He flung himself down upon the dead, silent camel, setting up a wailing every bit as piercing and heart-rending as his animal's screams had been. His palms stroked the beast's eyelids, with their long womanly lashes, and shut its widely spaced eyes, from which all signs of life had now departed. Then, calm and dignified, he got to his feet, walked over to the next body and broke down again, lamenting loudly before closing the animal's eyes. He repeated this ritual for every one of the camels, taking plenty of time. Preising held his breath, and a great sadness overcame him.

While Preising was reading his paper, the driver had left him alone and gone to join the others. 'That was a relief,' Preising admitted, 'because the surge of emotion that took hold of me at that point can rapidly become embarrassing in the presence of a stranger.'

Saida's chauffeur and the coach driver walked round the

metal elephant, appraising the damage with a professional eye, inspecting the dented radiator grille and making a half-hearted attempt to lever the dangling front bumper back into place; they even used their combined muscle power to tug at the dead camel's leg poking out from the wheel arch. The chauffeur then exchanged a few words with Saida before coming back to the car. He was breathing heavily as he sat back behind the wheel.

'I'm not in the habit,' said Preising, 'of getting involved in other people's business, but the caravan leader's despair and grief had touched such a raw nerve in me that I felt unable to maintain the cool detachment that might be expected of me when faced with these incomprehensible and alien events. And so I asked the driver, who spoke excellent French by the way, to fill me in on the situation. It was, he informed me, a really bad business, but the camel driver only had himself to blame – when all was said and done, there was a good reason why it was strictly forbidden to drive camels along the road, and as he came over the brow of that hill, the coach driver wouldn't have seen the animals until it was far too late. Saida was livid. For one thing, the bus belonged to Ibrahim Malouch, a cousin of Slim's, and the camel driver was bound to be uninsured, plus the passengers had been guests at Mr Malouch's desert resort, and now they were going to miss their return flights, forever casting a dark shadow in their memories over their stay at the Tschub Oasis. But worst of all, other hotel guests would now be waiting in vain for the desert camel trek they'd booked, as these were the camels in question. She had no idea, she said, who'd be able to take over the hotel camel-ride operation at such short notice.'

As Preising and the driver lapsed into silence and sat watching the road ahead, some of the men grabbed the camels' feet and started dragging them off the carriageway, while the camel owner sat in the dust by the roadside, his upper body wrapped in a white cloth, and rocked back and forth, staring blankly at the scene.

Le pauvre, il est ruiné. Complètement. He'd never bounce back from this, the driver meant. All his camels wiped out at a stroke. His livelihood gone, just like that, and with it a large family's sole source of income. *Complètement ruiné.* What would one of these camels be worth, Preising wanted to know. Eleven hundred, maybe twelve hundred francs, came the reply. Times thirteen.

Preising did a quick mental calculation: fourteen, fifteen thousand francs. Was that all it would take to rescue this man's – this whole family's – existence? He was completely beside himself.

'So there was this man, slumped in the dust right before my eyes, weeping over the loss of his camels, and of his livelihood, and all for just fifteen thousand francs. Fifteen thousand, that was the sum Prodanovic had once proudly presented me with at a press conference to announce annual results. Fifteen thousand francs, that was how much I earned at the firm each and every day. And that was just from my company shareholdings, leaving aside my salary as executive director, the interest from my other investments, my property portfolio, and all my many other sources of revenue. Fifteen thousand francs a day – an amount that meant life or death to this man. So what was stopping me from just getting out of the car, walking over to him and handing him the money, so he could buy himself a new string of camels? What was stopping me?'

I didn't have the faintest idea what prevented him from going over to the man and presenting him with this money, but I felt sure he was about to tell me. Preising could always find reasons for not taking action.

'Two things,' he explained, 'Prodanovic and Saida. Wouldn't my hostess construe such a gesture on my part as an affront? As unwarranted interference? Hadn't precisely the man whom I was planning to shower gifts upon just caused her untold trouble through his carelessness? What sort of impression would it make if I then went and rewarded him? This was a difficult situation that required careful thought. Suddenly, I called to mind the annual charity committee meetings chaired by Prodanovic, where we'd donate one percent of company profits to good causes like foreign aid projects or arts sponsorship. Every year without fail, Prodanovic refused point-blank to send even a single Swiss franc to Africa. The continent was drowning in Western aid, Africa was paralysed by charity donations, he contended. This continent would have to pull itself out of the mire by its own bootstraps. I seemed to recall that Prodanovic was mainly referring to sub-Saharan Africa. But didn't the same apply to Tunisia? Wouldn't I be effectively paralysing this man if I gave him money? Depriving him of the possibility of clawing his own way out of his misery, standing on his own two feet and carving himself out a bright future through his own enterprise? Yet one glance at the heaving shoulders of the sobbing man was enough to tell me that help really was required in his case, Prodanovic or no Prodanovic. Even at the risk of upsetting my hostess. It was going to cost me so little, and I was in a position to make such a huge difference. I'd made up my mind. Of course, I didn't have fifteen thousand francs in cash on me, in fact I had barely twenty-six thousand Tunisian dinars in my wallet. Maybe I should ask him to write down his account number so I could transfer the money to him? But would he even have a bank account? Or should I simply drive him to the nearest camel market and buy him thirteen new camels? Would I be able to pay with my credit card at a Tunisian camel market, though?'

Preising's agonised wrestling was cut short by Saida, who sat down beside him, apologised briefly for the disruption and told the chauffeur to drive on. Despondently, he was whisked past the stranded bus, the dead camels and their unfortunate owner, whose fate still preyed on his mind. In no time, the extensive date-palm plantations around the Tschub Oasis came into view. The desert wind was shaking their dark green crowns, making them look from a distance like ripples on the surface of a cool lake.

2

THE *THOUSAND AND ONE NIGHTS RESORT* in the oasis at Tschub was modelled on a nomadic Berber settlement – or, to be more precise, on what market researchers thought a first-class tourist to Tunisia might imagine when he pictured a typical Berber settlement. Assuming, that is, he could picture such a thing at all and wasn't, impartial as a blank sheet of paper and receptive as an empty vessel, simply being spoon-fed ideas by a world-renowned resort designer from Magdeburg. Sturdy white tents were liberally distributed around the bright palm grove. Various stone buildings, housing restaurants and bars, were concentrated around a natural rock pool, forming a picturesque ensemble. The whole compound was enclosed on three sides by a whitewashed wall topped with shards of broken bottle glass.

Yet without a doubt the *pièce de résistance* was the spa complex built into the sandstone bluff enclosing the northern perimeter of the oasis, in caves that had most likely once been used to keep camels' milk or other such provisions cool. They'd been dug out by hand at a time when this place had been inhabited by people who weren't either on holiday or earning a living from holidaymakers. But the day finally came when those people found themselves faced with the stark choice of either giving up their life of farming and herding in favour of a job at Slim Malouch's resort or upping sticks and going somewhere else, which usually meant moving into a cramped apartment in Tunis, Sfax or Gabès with all their nearest and dearest and hoping that at least one family member found work – for instance, soldering electronic components for European firms with dynamic and exotic-sounding names like *Prixxing*. The only other option was to scrape together every last cent and put it on a horse, usually ridden by the feistiest and most frustrated of the family's sons. In this case, the horse was actually a boat, barely seaworthy and invariably overladen with other migrants. But anyone who survived the crossing might manage to scratch a living in Europe and put enough by at the end of every month to send back home. And if he was to remain in his adopted country and find a wife who reminded him of home and have children with her, then maybe a guy like Prodanovic would turn up one day at the kids' school as a guest speaker and give them a rousing pep talk. Assimilate and succeed, who dares wins … you can be a winner, too! Yes, even you!

In any event, Preising was really impressed by the spa.

'Notwithstanding my aversion to sharing a room with total strangers when I'm sweaty and naked, I still hadn't entirely ruled out the possibility of having a spa treatment and using the steam-room cave one cool desert night. Especially as everything seemed to be quite correct and above-board; most of the guests I encountered on my brief recce had covered themselves very discreetly with large white Egyptian cotton bath towels.'

The other guests were mainly English. Preising quickly ascertained that almost all of them belonged to one large group. Numbering maybe sixty or seventy, they'd taken over most of the luxury tents. He wouldn't have identified them as a coherent unit, though – they were just too motley a bunch – if he hadn't, just a few hours after arriving, got to know someone who'd initiated him into the finer points of the resort's social hierarchy.

'I'd just sat down with a book on the Terrace of the Beys – at least, that's what Pippa, my new acquaintance whom I'll tell you about presently – and I soon christened the place; it was a little terrace up on the hill above the spa, which you could get to by climbing a flight of steps hewn into the bare rock, and on it there was a kind of Oriental four-poster, a wooden frame with carved posts and white drapes, which was equipped with an incredibly comfortable mattress and masses of cushions of every shape and size, all in pure white. Perched up there, just above the tops of the palm trees, you could enjoy a panoramic view of the desert and even catch a cooling breeze now and then. Anyway, I'd just ensconced myself there when I heard the sound of bare feet ascending the stone steps. I sat up immediately; having thought I was going to have the place to myself, I'd made myself at home and sprawled indecorously all over the mattress and cushions. Peering over the top of my book, the first thing I saw was a well-groomed short hairstyle, flecked with silver. Its owner was a woman around my age, who'd evidently found it a bit of a struggle getting up the steep steps, given that she was balancing a heavy water-jug and glass in one hand

and holding a pair of nearly-new-looking leather sandals with toe-loops in the other, all the while trying not to drop the book she had wedged under her arm. It was doubtless these trying circumstances that caused her mask of composure to slip for an instant when she caught sight of me, and she shot me a look of undisguised frustration; like me, she'd obviously sought this place out for its solitude. In any event, she quickly pulled herself together, greeted me with scrupulous courtesy, put her jug and glass down on the little side table, and with a tentative "May I?" sat herself down on the opposite side of the mattress without waiting for my reply. She crossed her legs, opened her book and, paying me no further heed, buried her nose in it. We both affected looks of studied concentration, since it was clear that neither of us were the kind of people who were used to sharing a mattress with a stranger.

'However, when I put my book aside for a moment to wipe my sunglasses, I saw her steal a sideways glance at what I was reading. "We seem to have the same interests," she said, holding up her own book to show me the dust-jacket. We were both reading Mahmoud Messadi's *The Birth of Oblivion*, she in an English translation and I in the German. My bookseller recommended it to me when I told her about my trip to Tunisia. She said it was the most important work of modern Tunisian fiction, in fact of modern Arab literature as a whole.

'Books are a wonderful ice-breaker. We began chatting away quite happily, swapping notes on our shared reading-matter. She was enthralled by Messadi; I hadn't made up my mind yet, but she was already quite a bit further on than me. Then, suddenly, she took off her dark glasses, revealing eyes of a quite strikingly intense blue. Truth be told, that was the only really notable thing about her appearance. She was of medium build with an unremarkable figure. She'd lost any girlish svelteness around the hips and tautness in her upper arms, and had one of those expensive-looking hairdos that educated Northern European women get when they feel they've grown too old for long hair. She was wearing barely any make-up and her clothes spoke of good taste and a total lack of vanity. Cotton, linen, presumably from an environment-friendly manufacturer. "Philippa Greyling," she said, holding out her hand, "but call me Pippa, please.""

It was the English teacher Pippa Greyling, then, who initiated Preising into the social standing of the various guests at the desert resort. When he recounted it to me, he tossed in an apposite quotation from *Anna Karenina* which summarised the social hierarchy in that little German spa where the Shcherbatskys go for a rest-cure.

What really made Pippa and Preising click straight away was the fact that they were both at the *Thousand and One Nights* under duress. She was here because her son had decided to hold his wedding at a Tunisian oasis resort, flying in no fewer than seventy friends and family members. That, Pippa explained, making no attempt to hide her irritation, was what a young couple who both worked in the City imagined passed for a society wedding. Her son Marc and his bride-to-be Kelly formed the nucleus of that large group whom Preising had already seen gathered round the pool. Young people in their late twenties or early thirties. Brash and self-confident. Trim and gym-toned. The men sported sand-coloured chinos, polo shirts and moccasins, and the women tank-tops and figure-hugging shorts over golden-tanned, silky-smooth legs. Flip-flops on their dainty manicured feet. Those who'd opted for a dip in the pool were wearing the kind of swimming trunks familiar from old photos of JFK on the beach at Martha's Vineyard, or skimpy bikinis that showed off flat stomachs to best effect and justified the Brazilian they'd had done before coming away. Even in this state of near-nakedness, though, they all looked like they were in uniform. Preising kept running into little knots of them all over the complex. He'd encounter them standing around one of the bars cracking jokes or disappearing, snogging furiously and groping each other under the waistbands of their tight shorts, into their climate-controlled tents, or ordering the staff around imperiously and stomping their way through the palm grove, cursing as they searched for better reception for their Blackberrys – after all, their salaries were such as to require that they should be contactable wherever they were, 24/7. Preising was astonished that the City could spare fifty of its young guns in the present climate. Maybe, he thought, the game was up already and they'd taken refuge here. Preising was tickled by this idea, and shared it with Pippa to try and cheer her up, but all it elicited was a contemptuous snort, which for one alarming moment he thought might be directed at him until he realised with relief that she was gazing at the rabble who'd assembled at the southern end of the pool.

The social gradient, as she put it, started at the northern end. That was where Kelly's brothers and sisters, who'd also been invited, had withdrawn to with their children. The kids, in loud-patterned trunks, kept hurling themselves into the pool and clambering out again, over and over, hollering and shrieking all the while; perched on the edge, their mothers were annoyed by the incessant splashing, which had wrinkled the pages of the women's magazines they were reading. After a few failed attempts to fraternise with the City Boys, Kelly's brother Willy, his chest turning red from the Tunisian sun, had taken refuge in a large yellow swimming ring, where, with the aid of a couple of bottles of Heineken, he now lay basking and trying to fathom how he should be feeling vis-à-vis the luxury surrounding him, for which he had his sister and new brother-in-law entirely to thank, and which he'd never be able to afford for his family off his own bat. He'd made it through the first day with an overwhelming sense of revulsion. That had given way to a studied serenity. Different world, he thought. Even a different planet. Planet of the Apes. He really did find them apish, too, the young people at the far end of the pool. The Young Ones: his private name for them, though in fact they were all much the same age as him. Then again, what did they know about the real world? He had three kids to provide for. And he liked his swimming trunks with the tattoo pattern.

'My husband', Pippa told Preising, 'only went to the pool once. Just long enough to formulate the theory that, with this generation, you can tell people's incomes from the colour of their swimming trunks.' According to him, the more garish they were, the more likely their owner was to be in the red. 'Sanford's a sociologist, you see,' she added apologetically. In fact, Pippa had really been hoping she might get to know Kelly's parents a bit better here, as she hardly knew them. But Mary and Kenneth Ibbotson had found it hard making the transition from Liverpool to Tschub – or maybe from their respective roles, as a shop steward in a machine-tool factory and a housewife, to the bride's parents at a £250,000 wedding – and were spending most of the time holed up in their air-conditioned tent.

'It was plain to see', Preising impressed on me, 'that Pippa was unhappy. Unhappy with her son's choice of career and his social circle, and with the fact that this wedding was being held in a Tunisian luxury resort. But she had a friendly nature and a sharp mind, and put a brave face on her unhappiness. Still, I couldn't help but observe social convention and offer my warmest congratulations on her son getting married. She thanked me with a small, ironic laugh.

'In fact,' he went on, 'it was me who spoiled the cheerful atmosphere by asking if Marc was her only child or whether she'd had to go through all these elaborate wedding preparations several times before.

'No, she replied, Marc was her only child, at least the only surviving one. Her elder daughter Laura had been killed three years ago. Just off the North Cape of Norway, in the bowels of a Hurtigruten cruise ship, on which she'd been working as a librarian. Incinerated, Pippa continued, along with a couple of hundred Scandinavian crime novels and the complete works of Stendhal, which a faulty fan heater had set alight.

'The manner in which she described her daughter's death surprised me. It was like she was standing at a bar and regaling people with an anecdote about how she'd come by a particularly impressive scar or lost the tip of one of her fingers. But perhaps that's actually what it was like for her. Like the loss of a body part or an amputation as the result of a grotesque accident. For someone like me, who never had any kids,' Preising said, 'it's hard to imagine what it means to lose a child.'

He stopped by a small bench in front of the yellow wall. 'You, though,' he said without looking at me, 'know only too well what it means.' No, actually I didn't. Preising was mistaken. Just because you've experienced something, it doesn't mean that you know what it means. And I had no intention of learning how to fathom it. Some things are so senseless that there's no point trying to give them meaning. Preising sat down on the bench, with his feet planted parallel to one another in the gravel and his hands on his knees. He was giving me time to open up to him. He'd have a long wait. I didn't feel the slightest urge to unburden myself. 'Please,' I said, pulling up a wrought-iron chair for myself, 'go on with your story.'

He gave me a concerned look and then continued: 'Pippa told me she was having trouble imagining which group her daughter would have latched on to. Laura would probably have sat up here the whole day, she said. But in all likelihood, they wouldn't have been able to persuade her to come in the first place. Laura hadn't liked hot countries, or large gatherings, or even small ones for that matter. She really wasn't a very gregarious person. Which made it all the more astonishing to her parents when she suddenly announced she'd signed up as a librarian on a ship, and would be plying up and down the Norwegian coast on the Hurtigruten run for a whole year. And Laura, Pippa added, just couldn't understand her brother's choice of career. She couldn't be doing with people who were obsessed with money.

'All things considered, this struck me as a very intriguing description of a young woman, and I could well picture Laura as her daughter. As I got the impression, said Preising, that Pippa liked talking about her daughter, I probed a bit further. Well, I told her, young people often find it easier to say what they don't like than what they do – at least, I know that was the case for me when I was a young man. So did Laura know what she liked? Oh yes, replied Pippa – cold countries, bad weather, the works of WG Sebald, and difficult men. Saying this, she laughed.'

Then, at least according to Preising, they'd sat there in silence for some time. It was Pippa who revived the conversation, muttering some *bon mot* about the trouble with wedding receptions, which he couldn't now recall in detail, though he was adamant it was a very witty observation. Yes, she went on, it was a tricky business, especially if you weren't religious and had cut yourself off from any possibility of sanctifying your union in the sight of God, with all the traditional wedding rites. Preising found himself agreeing with her. Unfortunately, he confessed, he'd never got the chance to marry. That is, he'd never felt ready to take the plunge; that was a far more accurate reflection of the true state of affairs.

Preising treated Pippa to some wedding stories about friends of his, and she reciprocated with an entertaining account of her own nuptials. How she and Sanford, in a desperate attempt to avoid any suspicion of bourgeois respectability right from the outset of their marriage, had decided to hold their wedding reception in a community centre on Loughborough Estate, a council-house development in Brixton. The venue was a concrete pavilion in the shadow of looming tower blocks and despite being only ten years old at the time, it had already started to crumble; inside, it smelt of piss and old clothes. The place had been painted in bold colours by the town planners in the vain hope that it might one day become the hub of a vibrant, multicultural community and host parties on summer evenings where all the people from the surrounding tower blocks would congregate to share Pakistani, Caribbean, Ghanaian and Irish home cooking. In the event, all it had played host to were occasional gang-rapes by bands of local youths and the Salvation Army clothing handouts on the first Tuesday of every month. The inhabitants of the tower blocks, flabbergasted that anyone should want to celebrate a wedding in these surroundings, passed by shaking their heads in disbelief. Small, dark-skinned boys on bikes squashed their noses against the windows to watch the boisterous dancing. A Tibetan chef hired specially for the occasion tried to interest the guests in his tsampa and butter tea, but they were more enthused by the liberal quantities of free beer on tap and in no time got really plastered, because apart from the tsampa there was nothing else to eat, and it transpired that solidarity with the Tibetan people didn't go that far. The only upside, said Pippa, was that we soon found ourselves alone with just our friends, because our relatives, parents, grandparents, aunts and uncles all left the reception well before dark, not unreasonably fearing that they might get stabbed and mugged on the way to their cars.

Meanwhile, Preising had made himself comfortable on the bench. I'd have preferred to stroll on a bit further, but he was right. After all, where were we supposed to go? To the far end of the yellow wall, where the porter would eyeball us suspiciously from his glass booth? And then back again to the other end, or along the gravel path that led past the rosebushes with their shiny red rosehips and past the fountain, only to run up against the yellow perimeter again? Plus, he'd get on better with his story sitting down, as he wouldn't feel the need to keep constantly stopping in his tracks and casting melancholy glances into the middle distance to lend weight to what he was saying – a middle distance which in any event was concealed from us by the high boundary wall. So, I let him be and ground my chair legs into the gravel to stop it rocking. Preising had taken off one of his slippers and swung his lemon-yellow-socked foot up onto his knee, rubbing it vigorously and revealing in the process an almost obscene expanse of pale shinbone, which for some reason I found myself transfixed by.

Massaging his heel, he picked up the thread of his story: 'Pippa and I were in stitches at that frank account of her wedding, and because I felt I ought to respond in kind, I told her the tale of my yurt in Biarritz. You know that one, don't you?' Here he shot me an inquiring look. Yes, indeed I did, I said, the one about the yurt in Biarritz and the chamber orchestra. It was etched on my memory, I assured him. 'Anyway, Pippa really enjoyed that one, and I followed up by remarking how pleasant it was at our age to look back on our youthful follies in the blissful knowledge that they were all now safely in the distant past. What do you mean "at our age"? she asked, with a flash of coquettishness. She teased me: how could I even say that when I still looked so youthful? I thanked her for the compliment and returned it suavely. That seemed to please her.

'Pippa steered our conversation back to literature. She had some fascinatingly profound insights into Arab writing, as it turned out. I listened to her, captivated, as she told me about the oral tradition and Mohamed Choukri and other writers whose names I forget and about Paul Bowles in Tangiers, who had recorded some of their stories on tape and then transcribed them while eating hashish jam from a jar. And in no time we were drinking from the same glass like old friends; I'd forgotten to bring one up for myself, you see.'

Preising's tête-à-tête with the fascinating Englishwoman was abruptly interrupted by the arrival of Sanford, Pippa's husband, who came bounding up the steps to the Terrace of the Beys. The sudden appearance of this wiry man in a white shirt and khaki shorts made Preising shoot up from his reclining position; even as he did so, he realised that made it seem as though he'd just been caught in a compromising position, but in actual fact it was just a reflex born of Preising's former acquaintance with another sociologist – or had he been an ethnologist, he was no longer sure – whose sharp tongue he feared more than the shell-suited young men who used to practise a sport called 'Ultimate Street Fighting' in a cellar opposite the head office of *Prixxing*.

But his fears were completely unfounded. Sanford was grateful that his wife had found someone to talk to. It salved his guilty conscience, after he'd abandoned her for the entire day to go and visit the ruins of an old desert fortress. A few pleasantries were exchanged, with the Englishman enthusing over his excursion and even inviting Preising to join him on another trip the next day, 'and of course, I'm still hoping you'll join us, my dear', he added, turning to his wife. But now it was time to freshen up for dinner. Would Preising care to join them for the evening? Sanford was sure they could make room for him on the long table, and they'd both be relieved, he said with a sideways glance at his wife, to have someone to chat to who was more on their wavelength.

Yesterday, Sanford explained, he'd listened with astonishment to a monologue from the person sitting next to him, a woman barely in her thirties who worked as a securities trader, who'd insisted on telling him at epic length about the happiest day of her life. The gist of it was that she'd gone down to a place called Zuffenhausen, in the south of

Germany as far as he knew, to collect a sports car straight from the factory. She'd been able to afford it thanks, as she put it, to an 'above-average annual performance with commensurate bonus', and she'd been in seventh heaven driving her new car back to England on German autobahns with no speed limit. It had been a real adventure, she was at pains to stress, because it was pretty disconcerting to be jockeying a right-hand-drive car at high speed through unfamiliar right-hand traffic; on several occasions, she claimed, it was only her amazingly sharp reflexes, honed by all those hectic hours on the trading floor, that had enabled her to cheat certain death. Fortunately for him, Sanford confided, he could listen to this kind of stuff with his professional hat on and think of it as background research. Of course, from a professional point of view, any prejudice was to be frowned upon; still, he couldn't help but observe that the truly striking thing about these people was the sheer gusto with which they fulfilled every stereotype in the book.

Preising regretted he'd have to decline their invitation, as he was due to have dinner with Saida. But he accompanied the couple through the palm grove to the tents. Sanford strode ahead in his trekking sandals, kicking up little dust clouds that settled in the blond hairs on his calves.

'In my tent', Preising said, 'whose interior bore not the slightest resemblance to a tent and was completely decked out with expensive Berber carpets, I finally got round to unpacking my bags. As I did so, I silently cursed my housekeeper, dear lady that she is.' Stroking his yellow sock with his thumb, he paused for a moment, dwelling on his housekeeper, before continuing: 'You see, she'd packed almost exclusively light-coloured clothes. Most of them sand-coloured and functional. You could have kitted out Rommel's Afrika Korps with the contents of my suitcase. Right at the bottom, lightly crumpled, I found my seersucker suit, which a nice young lady of my acquaintance had once bought me for a garden party in the Hamptons. It was completely inappropriate attire for dinner at a Tunisian oasis, but at least I wouldn't look like I'd stepped straight off the set of *The English Patient*. In any case, I didn't have a choice, as I'd bought two bottles of rose water at the souk in Tunis as small gifts for my housekeeper and my secretary, and one of them had leaked in my suitcase on the drive out to Tschub, leaving unsightly pink stains on all my other jackets.'

So, Preising shaved and put on his seersucker suit. He teamed it with a white shirt with a starched collar, which the rose water had only stained the back of. Standing in front of the mirror with the oriental frame, he buttoned and unbuttoned the second-to-top button of his shirt five times, casting a critical eye over his appearance each time until finally, with his eyes shut, he managed to perform a complicated manoeuvre with his left hand which left it entirely to chance whether the shirt ultimately remained buttoned up or not.

Preising left his tent and walked through the palm grove, which was already shrouded in darkness and only sparsely lit by a few lanterns. The leathery fragrance of his aftershave mingled with the cloying sweetness of rose water. White chest hairs sprouted out of his open collar. Even from some way off, he could hear the loud guffaws of the young people. He was sweating.

'I was seated at a small table near the bar, where I waited for Saida. Pippa waved at me from the long table that ran the whole length of the building. Sanford was sitting next to her clutching a glass of beer and listening to a young woman sitting opposite him, who was leaning right across the table towards him and punctuating her monologue with chopping hand gestures. Even from my distant vantage point, it was noticeable how revealing her Little Black Number was. I assumed she must be the Porsche driver.

'Saida came into the dining room, checking in passing at the odd table whether everything was in order, personally greeting the bride and groom, and finally apologising to me profusely for her late arrival. Our meal was, how shall I put it – well, the food itself was first-rate, but the occasion reminded me uncomfortably of that hour when Moncef Daghfous had left me in the care of his daughters while he dashed off to his phosphate factory to fire-fight with a shovel and a bucket of sand. It wasn't Saida's fault, she really made an effort, but somehow it was there between us on the starched damask tablecloth the whole time, the fact that this shared meal was just part of an assignment that her father had given her. I ventured some small talk. We chatted for a while about Paris, where she'd been a student. You know, I told her, in my youth I spent some time studying in Paris, too. And I started telling her about my wild Parisian days, but Saida was a serious-minded young woman who had no time for wild times. She really liked Lake Geneva, where she'd attended a famous school for hoteliers, so I mentioned Nabokov, whom she hadn't heard of, and his interest in lepidoptery, but butterflies cut no ice with her either. I took my leave as soon as I reasonably could, telling her what an eventful day I'd had and how tired I was.'

3

'NEXT MORNING, I was up bright and early as always, you know my routine. And if I suspect a breakfast buffet's going to be laid on, I make it even earlier. Just a hint of the coolness of the desert night still lingered in the morning air. I found Sanford sitting all alone at a table, already supplied with tea and poached eggs. Glancing over the top of yesterday's edition of an English newspaper, he prophesied: 'this'll all end in tears, you know. These kids, they'll be the ruin of us all, and Jenny won't even be able to afford the petrol for her Porsche.' Sanford dripped egg yolk over a photo of the fracas in idyllic Ilfracombe and shook his head in anxiety. He'd made up his mind, he went on, suddenly changing the subject, to go and see the ruins of some traditional Berber cave dwellings today, and would I like to come with him?'

Preising hesitated for an instant, avoiding committing himself straight away by quizzing Sanford about these mysterious places. They were underground homes, apparently, carved out of rocky hillsides and only accessible down long tunnels. They were hundreds of years old, but very little was known about them. Now everything was crumbling and collapsing, though, and in a few years' time they'd be swallowed up entirely. You could say it's our last chance to see them before they vanish forever, Sanford gushed.

Preising's enthusiasm for the trip took a sudden nosedive.

It all sounded far too unpredictable, too much like an adventure, and Preising, who prided himself on being able to read people pretty well, thought he could detect behind Sanford's façade of the cultivated academic a whiff of recklessness and a tendency to make snap decisions. That made him nervous. 'Come on,' Sanford cajoled him, 'It'll be an adventure!' Exactly, Preising thought to himself, that's just what I'm worried about. But on the other hand, how could he know what an English sociology professor's idea of an adventure was? Maybe it would be exactly the kind of adventure that would appeal to him too? Something more by way of an intellectual enterprise; to boldly go into uncharted hermeneutic territory, that kind of thing. But why, then, did Sanford need so many pockets on his trousers? Anyone who simply meant to let their mind wander far and wide from the comfort of a 4×4's interior would have no need of such things.

His musings were interrupted by a chirpy Saida, who poured herself a cup of coffee from the buffet and breezed over to their table to ask how Sanford was feeling on this most auspicious of days. Marc and Kelly's big wedding reception was to take place that evening. Sanford shrugged that off, and started to tell Saida about his and Preising's trip to find the last remaining troglodyte dwellings. Her face registered alarm; she'd get Rachid to go with them as a guide, she said. Sanford declined, Saida insisted, but Sanford continued to dig his heels in. He'd spent the past three days driving around the area on his own, and besides he was well equipped with local maps, plus the car he'd used had a SatNav, which was complete overkill. Saida wasn't persuaded; Sanford clearly felt patronised. In an attempt to defuse the situation, Preising chipped in that it might well be an advantage to have someone with them who knew the lie of the land. Yes, Sanford replied, that was all very well, but Rachid was the resort's pool attendant, a perfectly nice young man for sure, but he'd grown up on the outskirts of Sfax, and besides he was too chatty, he could talk the hind legs off a donkey. At this point, Saida put her foot down: Rachid was going with them and that was final, otherwise she'd stop them from using the hotel's pick-up. Sanford still wasn't about to concede defeat, and started to tell her he was perfectly capable of looking after himself, but Saida cut him short: 'I do not care what you do, Professor, but Mister Preising is in my responsibility. Take Rachid with you or join your family at the pool.' For a moment, Sanford was rendered speechless; just long enough for Saida to wish Preising a good day and sweep off.

Sanford flung his paper down on the table; his irritation led him to observe, chauvinistically, that Western-ers might need to revise their view of the traditional role played by women in Muslim societies. For his part, Preis-ing was impressed by Saida's assertiveness and incisiveness. Plus, she clearly felt responsible for him; somehow he found that gratifying. He could now set off on this jaunt with the Englishman and the pool attendant from Sfax in the certain knowledge that, during her busy day, which would be mainly taken up with preparations for the wedding feast, a little bit of Saida's attention would be focused on him and his safety. When he imagined her sense of relief – carefully concealed, of course, beneath her stern exterior – at seeing him return safely to the hotel at dusk, covered in dust, he found himself basking in a warm glow of pleasant anticipation.

When Preising duly appeared at the Toyota pick-up, wearing a narrow-brimmed fly-fisherman's hat and sand-coloured trousers – to be on the safe side, he'd chosen the pair with the most pockets, though both knees had unsightly rose-water stains on them – Rachid, a narrow-hipped man with broad shoulders, was loading a cool-box onto the back. The pool attendant was in high spirits and looking forward to the trip. Sanford scowled as he got Rachid to hand him the car keys and pointed inquiringly at the cool-box. 'Provisions', Rachid said, opening the plastic lid proudly, as though he was showing off a litter of puppies. The box was full to the brim with stuffed flatbreads, polystyrene tubs of all kinds of salads and sweets, plus any amount of bottled water. Enough to provision a major expedition. Sanford, who'd made up his own roll from the breakfast buffet and stuck a couple of bottles of water in his rucksack, gave a contemptuous snort and eased himself into the driver's seat. Preising and Rachid squeezed onto the narrow bench seat beside him.

'But just as Sanford was about to set off,' Preising continued, 'Rachid asked him to hold on for a minute so he could fetch his sunglasses. Sanford started the engine and glared out of the window as Rachid ran back inside to get them. All of a sudden, a wicked gleam came into his eyes. "Close your door," he told me curtly. I'd barely had a chance to do so when, to my astonishment, he stepped on the accelerator and shot through the delivery entrance and out onto the dead-straight dirt road. "What about Rachid!" I said, craning my neck to peer out of the narrow rear window of the pick-up at the nonplussed figure of the pool attendant, who was quickly lost in the cloud of dust we'd kicked up. Sanford, meanwhile, was acting like a teenager, yelping and whooping and punching the truck roof in triumph. I must admit, I got caught up in the mood and joined in his celebration of our little coup. Even so, my guilty conscience got the better of me, and I looked back once more. Imagine my shock when I saw, close behind us, with his chest puffed out and his arms extended right to the fingertips, pumping up and down and slicing through the dust-cloud like knives, a sprinting Rachid – what's more, he was clearly catching us up fast. "Step on it! Step on it!" I yelled, "he's gaining on us!" Sanford cursed, reminding me again of my sharp-tongued ethnologist and, glancing in the rear-view mirror, shifted up a gear and gunned the engine. He seemed to be taking the whole thing very personally now. Then again, so was Rachid, who kept powering on at speed through the dust-cloud, his chest heaving from the immense effort. Finally, we lost him, or in any event he disappeared from view in the billowing plume of dust. Sanford cackled hysterically for a while, then abruptly stopped and announced, not once but three times in quick succession, that he was perfectly capable of looking after himself and didn't need a guide. I was worried, though. A guide might well have come in handy and anyway, it was plain rude to blow off Rachid like that. Also, I'll admit, I was more than a little afraid of Saida's reaction. She'd take a pretty dim view of our high-handedness, that was for sure.

The only upside was that I was much more comfortable now – you know how I hate being hemmed in.'

In the event, hidden behind the vast dust-cloud that Sanford's frenzied style of driving had stirred up, and so unnoticed by him and Preising, Rachid dogged the truck for a full three kilometres. Sure enough, as Sanford had said, Rachid was the resort's pool attendant, but he was a pool attendant with a history. A history that began with a car crash on a slip road onto a motorway on the outskirts of Toulouse, which the eight-year-old Rachid was the sole member of his family to survive, and following which he'd been sent back to Tunisia to be brought up by his grandparents, who lived in Sfax.

His grandfather, a small man whose salt-tanned skin hung off his tiny frame like charred crepe paper, had been the last of the famous swimming harbour pilots of Sfax, though by the time little Rachid came to live with him, he'd long since been made redundant. Replaced by young men with state pilots' diplomas and steel-hulled boats to ferry them out to the freighters, rather than swimming out like Rachid's grandfather had done all his working life. In all weathers, even when the crests of the waves were towering over him, the height of a man, he'd keep on steadily making for the buoy with the big bell, which was anchored miles out in the Mediterranean and which he'd cling to, waiting for his allotted freighter, sometimes for hours on end. And when, finally, the huge bulk of the ship loomed up out of the darkness, he'd let the vessel's bow wave sweep him down its side, as his hands felt for the rope ladder. Catching hold of it, he'd climb up it as fast as he could and take up his post, wet and dripping, next to the helmsman, to guide him safely through the perilous shallows into the port of Sfax.

Rachid's grandfather, though, had had the misfortune to marry a cantankerous woman, so clinging to the yellow buoy and bobbing up and down in the water like a cork for several hours, occasionally switching the hand he used to grasp its rusty handle and treading water with a practiced economy of effort, didn't bother him in the slightest. In fact, he welcomed every opportunity to get out of his little house on the cliff and head for the open sea. Even though all that hanging about on the buoy only gave him plenty of time to mull over why his wife was so angry all the time. Sometimes, he fell to thinking that she was probably just unhappy, and if a freighter was badly delayed or the sea was particularly rough and the bell tolled especially loudly, he imagined that he was the one who was making her sad. Every so often he'd make up his mind, when he got back home, to ask her straight out why she was so miserable. And every time he resolved to do so, he had to make a conscious effort not to swim off that instant and go and confront her. As it happened, he never did swim back and ask her, because he was too afraid of what her answer might be.

When his only son was killed on that motorway in France, leaving him to look after his grandson, he'd long since given up swimming out to meet ships, yet things had got no better with his wife, and he hadn't found another job either. So he took to spending his days sitting on the breakwater with the other old, unemployed men, and whenever he sensed the little whitewashed house bearing down on him, feeling it almost breathing down his neck, he'd dive into the sea and swim out to the yellow buoy. It was no fun for Rachid being around his gloomy grandmother either, so he started to while away his time with the old men down at the harbour. He'd sit there trying to spot his grandfather's tiny head, with its grey hair, as it dipped and rose on the waves.

Presently, Rachid learned to swim himself; his grandfather taught him. In no time, he was swimming beside him, venturing further and further out before turning back and making for the shore on his own. When the old harbour pilot's wife died, he didn't give up swimming, as he often felt the need to reflect on why his wife had been so sad, and to curse himself for being such a cowardly old imbecile and never having the guts to ask her. When Rachid turned ten, they swam out to the buoy together for the first time. They bobbed around for a while in the warm water, clinging onto the buoy's rusty handles. But on the way back, Rachid began to tire and soon got into difficulties. He wrapped his arms round the wrinkled neck of his grandfather, who carried him all the way back. They only made dry land long after nightfall that day. Nothing like that would ever happen to Rachid again. Two days later they ventured out again, and he made it the whole way back unaided. From then on, they swam out to the buoy every day without fail, sometimes twice. Before long, Rachid was outstripping the old man.

One day, a scout from the Tunisian Sports Federation spotted him. Rachid was given a trainer and under his tutelage would spend hours on end swimming lengths in the Federation's big pool; nevertheless, he still managed to keep up his daily routine with his grandfather. At sixteen, he made the Tunisian national swimming team, and competed at two Olympics as well as several major international championships. Yet he never made the top three at big events held in indoor pools. His speciality remained long-distance sea-swimming, over twenty-five kilometres and more, feats of endurance that made him a local celebrity. First he became Tunisian champion, then African, and even made it on to the podium at one world championship. His grandfather went with him to most tournaments. Together, they toured the world's swimming pools: Schwäbisch-Hall, Fukuoka, Rome, Santa Fe, Helsinki. The old harbour pilot with the tanned hide finally keeled over and died poolside at the municipal swimming baths in Samara, three thousand kilometres from the ocean.

Rachid went back to Sfax and sold the little white house. He never wanted to see the sea again. Initially, he got a job picking dates at the Tschub oasis. When Slim Malouch took the place over, Rachid stayed on, working as a gardener at the *Thousand and One Nights* resort. But because he was the only one among the staff who could swim, he was soon given a pair of white trunks and reassigned as a lifeguard. Rachid was none too pleased by this move, but by now he'd got used to the desert and didn't want to up sticks again. Pretty soon, he came to realise that the pool of the *Thousand and One Nights* wasn't the sea, and after three years, when no guest had ever been in danger of drowning and no emergency arose which might have required him to enter the water – meaning that all he had to do was fish out the dead lizards with a long net first thing every morning – he came to terms with his new job as the pool attendant.

Even so, he was pleased when Saida entrusted him with the task of accompanying the two tourists on their desert trip.

At first it had just been a reflex reaction to run after the Toyota. But when Rachid saw the Englishman clench his fist in triumph, it became a competition. He kept chasing the dust-cloud for three kilometres. Sometimes he'd make up ground on them, only to see them pull ahead again. But they never managed to shake him off entirely. He felt like he could run for ever; his powerful lungs sucked in the hot desert air, he had limitless energy and staying-power, and he thought of his grandfather, the old pilot, and how they'd clung on to the buoy's rusty handles, and watched the big ships passing by far out at sea and heard the bell clanging above them to the rhythm of the waves, so loud that they just floated there in silence. Yes, he could run for ever; they'd never outdistance him. But then he remembered his sad grandmother, and a great wave of melancholy swept over him, forcing him to give up the chase at last. 'You fucking sons of whores!' he screamed at the receding tourists, before turning on his heel and jogging back towards the hotel.

'Although,' Preising resumed his story, 'we soon reached a tarmac road again, the journey was still really uncomfortable. Sanford did his best to be a pleasant and chatty travelling companion, telling me all sorts of interesting facts to do with the history of the Berbers. Still, I was relieved when, after two hours' driving, a small village came into view on a hillside and Sanford suggested we stop there for a glass of tea. In amongst the dusty hovels, we found a kind of village square with a little bar, whose metal tables and stools were covered by the shadow of the gendarmerie opposite.'

Sitting in the shade, Sanford started talking about the niceties of Berber village societies and the role played by women, and Preising, who'd read a bit about native peoples, chipped in from time to time. The sweet herbal tea put Sanford in a mellow mood, so he let it pass without demur when Preising started comparing the inheritance traditions of Guatemalan hill tribes with the bloody initiation rites of certain West African peoples – or was it the indigenous peoples of Surinam? – and made only a very tenuous connection between this and the Berbers. Suddenly, a window in the gendarmerie was flung open, directly above what remained of the chipped and battered coat of arms of the Republic, and a bald-headed policeman sporting a thick moustache and a gold *fourragère* appeared, holding a telephone to his ear. As Preising looked up, their eyes met. Always convinced that it was a good idea to keep on friendly terms with the local authorities, he gave the gendarme a cheery wave. In reply, the policeman raised two fingers to his bald forehead in a military salute, finished his phone conversation, pulled a pack of *Boussetta* out of his breast pocket and settled down at the window for a quiet smoke, with his gut resting on the sill.

In an attempt to get Preising's attention again, Sanford served up the tale of the traditional Tunisian wedding feast. This basically consisted of a roasted camel with couscous. But the camel, which was cooked whole, was supposedly prepared in the refined manner of a Russian *Matroschka* doll, being stuffed with a whole sheep, which in turn was stuffed with a goat stuffed with a bustard stuffed with a dozen quails, each of which had been stuffed with barberries and dates. Preising was sceptical. He had the feeling he'd heard this story, or something very like it, somewhere before, and in the context of a joke, what's more .

Before they'd finished their tea, indeed even before the moustachioed policeman had had a chance to finish his cigarette, a black 4×4 drew up in front of the gendarmerie. A young man in a dark suit got out of the passenger seat and disappeared into the building. Preising looked up at the window, but the smoking gendarme had vanished too. Soon after, the man in the dark suit reappeared, got back into the car and sat staring straight ahead through dark sunglasses. The driver kept the engine running.

Sanford paid for their tea, and they left the village on a narrow dirt track leading up into the mountains.

'Presently,' Preising continued, 'I got the impression a vehicle was tailing us. I don't mind telling you, the very thought brought me out in a cold sweat. I'd heard enough stories about kidnapped tourists.' Even recounting the incident now, his eyes still widened in terror, and to illustrate the dreadful anxiety that must have taken hold of him at the time, he gripped my wrist for a moment. 'I glanced across at Sanford and noticed that he kept looking in the rear-view mirror. He'd obviously spotted the car behind us, too.'

'Someone's following us,' Preising announced. Yeah, replied Sanford, it looked that way to him, too. 'See, what did I tell you!' Preising started to babble, 'if only we'd listened to Saida, we'd have Rachid with us now. Oh God, we should never have given him the slip…if only Rachid was here!' And what use did he think a pool attendant would be? Sanford wanted to know. He wasn't sure, Preising replied, but it'd obviously be an advantage having a local with them if they were kidnapped. 'Kidnapped? Who said anything about being kidnapped? Who by?' Sanford asked. Al-Qaida maybe, or Tunisian guerrillas fighting for independence, came the response. Sanford patiently explained that Tunisia had been independent since 1956 and then added: 'No need to go shitting yourself, my friend: it's the two suits in the 4×4 following us, and they're not about to abduct us.'

'Who are they, then?'

'Dunno, probably the TSWBS.'

Tee-ess-doubleyou-bee-es? Preising thought it had an ominous ring. 'What's that?' he enquired.

'Tunisian State Wankers in Black Suits,' replied Sanford, cackling uproariously.

If he hadn't been so petrified, Preising would have been genuinely shocked at Sanford's reply. He'd always imagined English academics' sense of humour to be as dry as dust and as black as night, but never anything less than refined.

'Chin up, old chap!' Sanford said, punching him play-fully on the thigh. 'Relax, they're from the state security department, the secret service – the SFNP, or whatever they call themselves here.'

'SFNP?' Preising asked distrustfully.

'Sadistic Fingernail Pullers,' Sanford hooted, whacking his palm down on the steering wheel in uncontrollable mirth.

'What do they want with us, though?' gasped Preising.

'Is it to do with these cave dwellings? Aren't we allowed to explore them or something?'

'No, they're here because of you,' Sanford grinned. 'I'm figuring the lifeguard snitched on us, so now your girl-friend's put state security on our tail so you don't go and get yourself lost. She really seems to have a thing for you. Looks as though she's well connected, too.'

They both looked up at the mirror. The 4×4 was still tailing them, keeping the same distance.

'Shall we try and give 'em the slip?' the adventuresome Englishman suggested.

'I found myself obliged to remind him of his responsibilities as a father, who couldn't possibly have any interest, just hours before his son's wedding – his only son, what's more – in smashing himself up in a pick-up truck at the bottom of a Tunisian ravine. As it happens, I'd have been better off not broaching the subject of the wedding, as it only seemed to make Sanford seriously consider the possibility of driving us over the precipice, either just in order to escape the impending ceremony, or because I'd inadvertently reminded him of the loss of his daughter Laura and triggered some death-wish in him.

'I was reading somewhere recently,' Preising told me, trying to sound casual, 'I can't remember exactly where, that the loss of a child can trigger panic reactions in the parents even years later, when they find themselves suddenly overcome by grief.' I purposefully folded my hands in my lap and stopped grinding my feet into the gravel to indicate to him that I was far from any such reaction, in the hope that he'd leave it at that and get back to his story. It worked; after shooting me one more concerned sideways glance, he picked up the thread again: 'Anyway, Sanford kept his foot to the floor, causing the rear wheels to skid across the dirt track every time we took a corner. Several times we only avoided plummeting over the edge by a whisker.'

Preising was only able to breathe easy again, he told me, when the mountain road reached a narrow plateau and ran on into the far distance almost as straight as a die. As for Sanford, now that he no longer had the means to kill himself close at hand, he seemed to lose interest in outrunning their pursuers and slowed to a leisurely pace, all the while scanning the barren but majestic landscape left and right for any signs of troglodyte dwellings. The dark 4×4 kept following them at the same distance, and when Sanford pulled over, their minders followed suit.

The English sociologist put on his backpack and insisted on going the rest of the way on foot. No one had told Preising he might need a rucksack, so he shoved two cold water bottles in the pockets of his walking trousers and tucked a couple of flatbreads inside his shirt. The grey, greasy marks they made formed a pleasing contrast with the rose-water stains on his trousers. He had trouble keeping up with the nimble Englishman, especially with the water bottles bouncing around in his pockets and the sun-block he'd hastily slapped on as they set off running into his eyes. He didn't think it prudent to ask his companion to slow down, as Sanford was already visibly irritated by the presence of the security men, who were only there in the first place because of Preising. His annoyance turned to open fury when, turning round to check on the progress of the stumbling Preising, he saw that their shadows were still in pursuit. The men hadn't even bothered getting out of their car to follow them on foot, but had simply driven their heavy 4×4 off the road and, steering it carefully round small rocky outcrops and rolling over clumps of thorny scrub, were trundling slowly after them like some large, grazing buffalo.

Preising managed to get himself in Sanford's good books again, though, when he spotted five low hummocks like the rims of craters on the gently sloping ground at the fringe of the high plateau, which Sanford immediately identified as the last remnants of a cave dwelling. The wiry sociologist broke into a trot, his trekking sandals slapping against his feet, and Preising scrambled after him as best he could.

'In the end,' Preising said, 'it turned out to be something of an anticlimax. I mean, all that kerfuffle – leaving the lifeguard stranded, the supposed kidnap, our helter-skelter drive round the ravine, and the strenuous tramp to the caves. Don't get me wrong; you know how keen I am on foreign civilisations, but after all the problems we'd had and the bother we'd caused, these cave dwellings were frankly a bit of a let-down. That may have had to do with the fact that we could only see the complex from outside, from above that is, as all the passageways down to the underground caves and central chambers had either collapsed or were barricaded by rough plank doors secured with heavy padlocks. Signs in Arabic and French forbade people from entering, with dire warnings about the danger of being buried alive. The signs, though, were immaterial to Sanford, I'm sure. The only thing that stopped him from picking up a rock, smashing open the rusty padlocks and going down to explore the underground complex was the presence of the security goons, who kept watching us from their vehicle through binoculars the whole time.'

Sanford, however, did not share Preising's disappointment. Far from it – he was ecstatic, peering down the dark passages through gaps in the plank doors, hurrying from one opening to the next and encouraging the exhausted Preising to scramble on all fours up the spoil heaps surrounding the underground chambers and gaze down into these clayey holes in the ground to catch a glimpse of the dark alcoves and rooms leading off them. He provided a running commentary on the lives of the Berber tribes who had inhabited these complexes centuries ago, pointing out the individual cooking niches, one for each woman in the tribe, and the rooms reserved for the men, and the areas where the livestock were kept. He also took masses of photos and even asked Preising to hold him by his belt so he could lean out further over the rim of one of the chambers to get a better angle for a shot.

So Preising took hold of the Englishman's greasy belt as he lay on his stomach and inched out dangerously far over the crumbling earth parapet. He found himself fascinated and indignant in equal measure at the completely hairless and astonishingly white and lean pair of buttocks that began to emerge, centimetre by centimetre, from the sociologist's walking trousers, just a hair's breadth above Preising's clenched knuckles gripping the leather. And now that her husband's half-bared backside was staring him in the face, it was just a short step for Preising to start imagining Pippa's bottom. The image this conjured up almost made his head swim, as all the blood rushed to his groin, partly because he was able to picture the English teacher's rear as extremely shapely – the presence of her husband only added to the excitement – partly because the effort of holding on to Sanford was making his breathing very strained – a feeling he remembered from gym classes at school, when they'd had to shin up a climbing pole – but also, to his astonishment, because he found himself not entirely unmoved by the sight of a half-naked male bottom under the North African sun. These unexpected and contradictory sensations were heightened still further by the knowledge that this was all unfolding under the field-glasses-equipped gaze of Tunisian state security, and his photographer companion's exhausted panting roared in his ears like a hurricane.

They spoke little on the homeward journey. Near the resort, they overtook a local dressed in a Manchester United shirt – No. 8, Rooney – who was leading a camel decked out in all kinds of finery. 'That's the camel for my daughter-in-law. She's going to ride to the altar.' 'On a camel?' Preising asked. 'That's right,' Sanford replied, 'on camel-back.'

4

PREISING'S HOMECOMING was far less triumphant than he'd imagined. Saida didn't look the least bit relieved to see him.

Fortunately, she was so busy with preparations for the wedding reception that she couldn't spare him more than a couple of minutes of her time. Even that was enough, though, to leave him feeling thoroughly shamefaced. Shamefaced and disillusioned, since she made it abundantly clear that his childish little escapade – she brushed aside his craven attempt to shuffle off responsibility onto Sanford – annoyed her not because she had any real concern for him but because it had caused her untold hassle. Plus – and this really seemed to rile her – it had cost her an awful lot, too; hurtfully, she hinted that the hospitality he was enjoying here was nothing more than an accounting item. As Slim Malouch's daughter, she intimated, she could always ask the state security services for a favour, but at the end of the day, they didn't come cheap. Quite the opposite, in fact, as payment was never in hard cash, but rather in the form of return favours. At some unspecified future date, there'd be a request for help of some kind or another, impossible to refuse. As such, the ultimate cost was incalculable.

Silently cursing the former instrument engineer Prodanovic, whose fault it was he was in this position, Preising slunk off, passing the former world long-distance swimming champion, who was crouching in the shadow of a wall playing with a skinny greyhound and her four boisterous puppies, and who pointedly ignored him as he walked by.

'After a refreshing shower, which wasn't nearly as cold as the verbal dousing I'd just been given, I grabbed my copy of Mahmoud Messadi, a jug of water with lemon and a basket of dates and climbed the steps to the Terrace of the Beys, where I found Pippa, who was staring intently at a piece of paper. She seemed really pleased to see me. Her husband had just been up to see her, she said, and had enthused about our trip. She told me she was delighted that I was going off with Sanford on his expeditions and keeping an eye on him for her, as he could be a bit reckless sometimes. I wasn't at all sure I'd fulfilled my role to her satisfaction. It struck me, rather, that I hadn't managed to tame Sanford's reckless streak in the slightest. I suppose at least I'd held him by his belt when he leant over the rampart to get better photos.

'Pippa invited me to sit down beside her, and I asked her how her day had been. She'd been trying, she told me, holding up the sheet of paper, to learn this poem off by heart. She was planning to recite it, as her contribution to the wedding celebrations that evening, but she was clearly finding memorising poems harder than she used to – a sign of advancing years, she supposed. No, really – she countered my protestations that that was quite out of the question where she was concerned – there was no escaping the fact that she'd once found it incredibly easy to commit poems to memory, though she'd found it even easier back then delivering them in public, something she felt increasingly uncomfortable about nowadays – she got the impression that the moments when poems were appropriate were getting fewer and farther between. I could only agree with that observation of hers. But, I said, all the more reason to fight tooth and nail against this deplorable trend. Poetry and reading it aloud were an essential part of life, it was what made us human beings.

'She wasn't sure she'd go that far, she replied, but she mentioned some long-dead American philosopher, whose name sadly eludes me now, who'd coined an idiosyncratic phrase for the skill of reading poetry in public –"to be able to rattle off some old chestnuts" – which struck both Pippa and me as being apt. Apart from conveying the sense of "quickly reciting", the term "rattle off" also conjured up the satisfying clonking noise two chestnuts make when you shake them around in your cupped hands. It was a brilliant image in so many ways, Pippa thought: the idea of rattling something off made no attempt to disguise the absurdity of having a poem ready to whip out and recite for every occasion, but on the other hand the chestnuts were a clear allusion to the autumn of life, the stage the American philosopher – why can't I remember his name? – was at when he wrote those lines, having apparently already been told he had a terminal illness. Plus, she continued, it stood to reason that reciting poems was something older people did, not those in the first flush of youth. Saying this, she gave a deep sigh and cast a melancholy glance at the sea of palm fronds at our feet.

'I felt genuinely sorry for her that she should suddenly feel herself on the slide towards old age just because her son was about to get married. Though I had to admit, these young people had a special talent for making everyone else feel old.'

That wasn't simply down to their unashamedly youthful appearance, though, as Preising mistakenly assumed. Their full heads of hair, their washboard stomachs, their slim hips. Nor was it even their laid-back attitude, their raucous behaviour, their studied playfulness, or the ironic undertone that accompanied their every utterance. No, ultimately it was due to their ability to pass off the game they were playing as deadly earnest. And of course, they could only manage to do that because the game itself was so high-stakes. Its potency lay in money, in the astronomical sums they dealt in daily, and in the obscene salaries they received. How could something with such a profound impact on society be treated as just a game?

Even Willy, drifting about in the yellow rubber ring after his third bottle of Heineken, had realised the futility of this whole enterprise. Where there's money, that's where the truth is, too. And that's why, mused Mary Ibbotson, the dusty taste of charcoal tablets still in her mouth, there's no common consensus about what you'll find at the end of the rainbow. On the Channel Islands, Mary knew from having a cousin on Guernsey, the saying went that you'd find the truth at the end of the rainbow, while at home in Liverpool an old nursery rhyme said it was a pot of gold. And because she didn't trust her analytical faculties, she didn't follow her train of thought through to the end, leaving her with the vague notion that you'd probably find both money and truth there. Or even more likely, that they were one and the same thing, so proving her cousin right. That made sense when she thought about it; after all, they knew a thing or two about money on Guernsey. Still, she put that thought to one side, because she'd never really got on with her cousin.

Nor was it just the Ibbotsons who were tormented by such thoughts. Sanford, who very much did trust his analytical faculties, couldn't help but come to the unsettling conclusion that a perverted society had spawned a perverted and debased version of William James' theory of 'cash value', a thought that sent a shiver down his spine. For if James was right to say that what is useful is true, and he didn't doubt it for an instant, then the problem of the ever-widening income gap, apparent since the days of Margaret Thatcher, didn't just have to do with an unequal distribution of wealth, but also with an unequal distribution of truth. In the context of society, that filled him with dread, while on a personal level it left him feeling that his life, his career and his convictions had all been marginalised, downgraded to the status of mere games. And, because he felt anything but young right now, these weren't children's games either, but OAPs' games, pointless pensioners' pastimes like sociology, golf, pétanque, communitarianism, and bingo: it all was all one and the same. In short, in the presence of his son and his friends, he seemed old. The same went for his wife, though she, being less inclined to analytical thinking, just got the distinct feeling that the broad-chested, slim-hipped new narrative of the financial markets had pronounced her English teaching, her book clubs and her passion for poetry useless.

Things were a bit different in Preising's case. If money was truth, then he had no shortage of truth on his side. And where financial clout was concerned, the prerogative of determining what should be seen as playful or serious was surely his. Why, then, did he feel so intimidated by the brimming self-confidence of all these derivatives traders and structured financial product development managers?

That's an easy one, I thought to myself, snatching up a handful of gravel, it's because Preising didn't know the first thing about money. It wasn't that it slipped through his fingers or that he squandered it or anything like that; on the contrary, he scarcely spent any, and that was what made his dealings with money so irresponsible.

In fact, he feared money in the same way he feared all tools. Of course he wasn't worried that he'd cut his fingers on it or catch something in it. No, Preising was afraid of the sheer efficacy of tools – he recalled with a shudder how, when skiing at Les Diablerets, he'd once watched two men cut through a cable for a new drag lift that was as thick as a man's arm using what seemed to him an impossibly small machine, though it could obviously exert massive lever-age. This set him thinking: when all was said and done, money was nothing but an especially effective tool, one that could smooth the path to greater and higher things, as Prodanovic had explained to me when he'd come to visit Preising last Friday and I'd been introduced to him.

Of course, Preising wasn't inclined to give too much

thought to greater and higher things, or at least he wasn't willing to do anything more than just think about them, and certainly wasn't prepared to shoulder the responsibility that came with them, and so sidestepped people's expectations of him on this score by simply contenting himself with being rich – stinking rich even, I presume. Otherwise, he led the life of an average citizen, apart from having a housekeeper, an extravagance he only allowed himself because she relieved him of the need to make various workaday decisions.

But ultimately, I thought, that was the thing about thinking. I seriously doubted, you see, whether Prodanovic expended much effort on it either. I suspected this despite only knowing him from Preising's anecdotes and from a brief encounter in the shadow of the yellow wall. Even so, I didn't reckon I was doing him any great injustice with this assumption, just placing him alongside his fellow movers and shakers and big-league earners, whose constant refrain, if you pressed them, was that money wasn't what drove them, and that they weren't just about amassing money for its own sake. It was as though they imagined someone might get the absurd idea that they tipped all the money they earned into a big hopper and spent all day dipping their rumps in it. No, no, according to them, money was merely a means to an end, it opened up possibilities, released the potential to achieve great things. Though this greatness was mostly measured in terms of the square meterage of living space in Cap Ferrat or the hull length of a luxury yacht moored at St Barth. Best of all, wealth gave you the wherewithal to acquire yet another bra-underwire factory in Bangladesh, which then generated more capital for them to 'set things in motion', as such people liked to put it. The fact that money didn't exist for its own sake was self-evident, that was the whole point of the stuff. But why did these people try to claim that they were the first to have realised this, and why did they imagine it would make anything better?

The state of fury I'd now thought myself into rendered me incapable of sitting on my garden chair a moment longer. 'Right, come along then,' I brusquely told Preising, dropping my handful of gravel and getting to my feet.

Preising, who thought I was referring to his story rather than our walk, struggled to pick up the thread again.

'So, anyway,' he said at length, 'Pippa seemed a bit down in the mouth, so I tried to cheer her up by asking her what poem she'd chosen to recite at her son's wedding. It turned out to be a longish piece by an American poet called Snyder, who was unknown to me at the time and, it seemed to me, somewhat obscure. He was a Beat poet, a Zen Buddhist and a co-founder of the Deep Ecology movement in the States. A pretty eclectic mix, I think you'll agree. Anyhow, because I didn't know it, I asked her to read it aloud for me. She hemmed and hawed for quite a while before finally giving in and reciting the poem in a wonderful British accent.'

He suddenly skipped ahead of me and, turning and blocking my path, took a deep breath before solemnly intoning:

Axe Handles
by Gary Snyder

'You see,' he interjected, 'I know it off by heart; during the turmoil that occurred the following day – which I'll tell you about presently – I had the presence of mind to pocket Pippa's sheet of paper with the poem on, which saved it from the flames. It's my only memento of this whole adventure, and I've looked at it so often that I can now recite the whole thing from memory.' So saying, he spread his arms wide – I'm not sure whether this was meant to stop me escaping or to lend his performance more gravitas – and launched into his recital. With his strong Swiss-German accent every '*the*' came out as '*sse*'; nevertheless, he still managed a passable impression of his English-teacher friend:

> One afternoon the last week in April
> Showing Kai how to throw a hatchet
> One-half turn and it sticks in a stump.
> He recalls the hatchet-head
> Without a handle, in the shop
> And go gets it, and wants it for his own.
> A broken-off axe handle behind the door
> Is long enough for a hatchet,
> We cut it to length and take it
> With the hatchet head
> And working hatchet, to the wood block.
> There I begin to shape the old handle
> With the hatchet, and the phrase

First learned from Ezra Pound
Rings in my ears!
"When making an axe handle
the pattern is not far off."
And I say this to Kai
"Look: We'll shape the handle
By checking the handle
Of the axe we cut with—"
And he sees. And I hear it again:
It's in Lu Ji's Wen Fu, fourth century
A.D. "Essay on Literature"– in the
Preface: "In making the handle
Of an axe
By cutting wood with an axe
The model is indeed near at hand."–
My teacher Shih-hsiang Chen
Translated that and taught it years ago
And I see: Pound was an axe,
Chen was an axe, I am an axe
And my son a handle, soon
To be shaping again, model
And tool, craft of culture,
How we go on.

Up on the Terrace of the Beys, Preising found himself swept along by the metaphorical power of the American poet's work and utterly lost in the English teacher's strikingly blue eyes, overlooking in the process the deepening furrows on her forehead. After she'd finished, there was a moment's pregnant silence. The only sound was a faint rustling in the tops of the palm trees, until Pippa broke the spell with a short English oath that began with an 'F'. After his excursion with Pippa's husband that day, Preising believed himself *au fait* with the peculiarly coarse way in which the British academic class liked to express itself, and thought she must be signalling her strong approval of the sentiments in the poem she'd just read out. He himself was lost for words, as none of them seemed quite adequate to the occasion; he was, after all, operating in a foreign language. Finally, he ventured a tentative 'Yes, indeed …', only to break off immediately and try a different tack, informing her that 'the apple does not fall so far from the stem, as we say in Switzerland' and that Snyder's poem had captured that old adage perfectly.

Pippa thought his interpretation sold the poem a bit short, and gazed gloomily past him into the middle distance. Then it all began to spill out. She'd decided she wasn't going to make a spectacle of herself at the reception; what had she been thinking of? It was obvious that in shaping her axe handle, she'd taken some duff measurements, with the result that she couldn't remotely assume that her son would get the subtle message of the poem, let alone share her love of poetry; after all, they didn't share a passion for anything else. And now it was clearly a bit late in the day to start trying to teach him. They – she expressly included Sanford in her recriminations – had just made too many mistakes bringing him up. They hadn't succeeded in passing on the things they found important. Preising said nothing. The whole situation, she continued, could be read in one of two ways – either she'd shaped him badly, or she'd failed to provide him with a good enough model. The first seemed the more likely, since she couldn't see anything of her in her son at all. In any case, she was adamant that reciting a poem at his wedding wasn't going to change a thing.

Preising felt it incumbent on him to say something to soothe the bitterness she was feeling. He appreciated how difficult it must be for her to see it now, he began – that surely had to do with the surroundings and the circumstances – but she'd doubtless taught her son far more than she gave herself credit for.

'Pippa,' he went on, 'remember, this poem goes way back in time, into the history of many generations, and also points the way forward to future generations. It reflects,' he continued, getting into his stride, 'the Great Chain of Being. One day, your son will become a father himself, and when he does, he'll think back on your words. It's really important, this poem. Pippa, you have to recite it this evening.'

She shot him a sceptical sideways glance. 'Do you really think so? I'll make myself a laughing-stock.'

'Not at all,' replied Preising, drunk on his own eloquence; in truth, he knew next to nothing about the relationship between grown-up children and their parents, 'go on, rattle off the old chestnuts!'

'Rattle off the old chestnuts?' The English sociology professor, who'd appeared quite unannounced on the terrace, was giving Preising a look of quizzical amusement, as though he'd just propositioned his wife with some improper but laughable suggestion. Preising immediately embarked on a convoluted explanation, made all the more confusing by his forgetting the name of the American philosopher, but was soon cut short by Pippa, who told her husband to stop browbeating their new friend.

Sanford, it transpired, had come up to the terrace to ask Pippa to go over a few last-minute details with Saida. Mrs Ibbotson was still feeling unwell and there was some confusion about the seating plan – matters that Saida was only prepared to discuss with the immediate family. Pippa refused at first, telling Sanford he could just as easily deal with it. At that point Sanford was forced to reveal that Saida wasn't particularly well disposed to him, though he glossed over why, saying she came across as a very difficult woman; difficult, and touchy with it. Pippa shot her husband a sceptical look, as Preising concentrated on fishing a slice of lemon out of his water glass. He was relieved that she left it at that. She stood up and kissed Sanford on his freshly shaved, scrawny neck. Before she left, she invited Preising to come along as their guest that evening, it would be her and Sanford's pleasure, and Kelly and Marc would be fine with it, too. Preising made his excuses – he didn't have the right clothes for such a grand occasion – but the couple reassured him the dress code would be quite casual; Sanford thought Preising's seersucker suit would do admirably. Just what an English wedding in the Tunisian desert needed, then: a Swiss businessman dressed like a plantation owner from the Deep South.

5

AT THE APPOINTED HOUR, Preising slipped once more into his seersucker suit. Putting it on reminded him of the astonishingly green lawn where the garden party in the Hamptons had been held, during which the young lady who'd invited him and bought him the suit for the occasion had got him drunk by plying him with a prodigious number of mint juleps served in chased silver goblets. He'd only managed to escape her blatant attempts to seduce him, with all the unforeseeable consequences that would have entailed, when, late in the day, one of the hordes of overtired and overexcited children present at the party, an eight-year old brat with a sharp crease in his trousers and size 34 penny loafers, accidentally smashed two of her toes with a croquet mallet.

His white shirt with the rose-water stains on the back smelt a bit high, after he'd sweated profusely in it the previous evening while trying and failing to interest Saida in Nabokov's butterfly-hunting excursions above Lake Geneva. He made a half-hearted attempt to mask the B.O. by splashing a liberal amount of aftershave under the arms, and as he did up his shirt he neatly sidestepped the tricky matter of the second button by forcing himself to count the number of circumflexes in Proust's famous passage about the madeleines. He'd taken the trouble to learn it off by heart in the original after noticing that the subject of childhood reminiscences about cakes, or food in general, tended to crop up a lot in social situations.

Thus kitted out, he left his tent, straightened his shoulders and strode through the palm grove in the direction of the noise coming from the poolside bar, where the wedding guests had already assembled to fortify themselves for the main event with champagne and tempura prawns served with harissa mayonnaise. Even from a distance, a lone braying laugh rang out above all the general hubbub of chatter and laughter. Preising had no trouble identifying it as belonging to a man he'd spotted early on, soon after his arrival here. He was a few years older than the rest, and the first thing that struck you about him was that he was the only one with a bit of a spare tyre, which he self-consciously flaunted beneath his broad chest. Preising had heard the others call him 'Quicky', yet in spite of this totally ridiculous name, they seemed to show him a certain respect, avoiding, for example, slapping him matily on the back. Conversely, though, they took it as a badge of honour when Quicky gave them a playful jab to the stomach, something he seemed fond of doing. He barked orders at the staff in a rudimentary Arabic. In unguarded moments, Quicky – who hadn't quite turned forty, Preising guessed – presented a weary face to the world, but otherwise put up a front of aggressive virility that Preising found unduly sexually charged and seamy. A hyena among tiger cubs, Pippa said, while Sanford dubbed him an 'arch-arsehole among common-or-garden arseholes' after seeing him do a cannonball into the pool clutching a bottle of beer in each hand.

'In these circles,' Preising told me, '"casual" clearly just meant taking off your tie and unbuttoning your jacket. The young men were all wearing slim-fit, made-to-measure suits with light shirts, dressed in exactly the same way as they went to work every day, except without their ties and with their top buttons undone. The girls wore floaty silk dresses from German fashion houses; their wide necklines slipped, as though unintentionally, off their bony shoulders, revealing brown collarbones that reminded me of grilled chicken carcasses. Their hemlines,' Preising told me, 'ended well above their knees, which were for the most part pretty knobbly, though lightly tanned.

Pippa looked enchanting, dressed in a sleeveless linen dress which cleverly picked out the colour of her eyes and formed a striking contrast with her greying hair. She introduced me to the Ibbotsons; a charming couple – I really enjoyed sitting with them under a large sunshade at a table set apart from the main throng of people and chatting animatedly about Liverpool. Mary Ibbotson drank lots of Perrier and said very little, while her husband, a taciturn trade unionist of the old school who was finding it hard coping with the heat, sipped on a glass of rosé champagne and tried to tempt his peaky-looking wife into trying a prawn, which he'd taken the precaution of scraping the spicy mayonnaise off first. After all, he told her, displaying that robust pragmatism typical of the working class, in the end it was just fish and chips, only without the chips. Then, finally, it was my turn to be introduced to Marc, who, wearing a dark suit and an open-necked shirt, had made his entrance at the poolside bar a few moments earlier, to loud cheers from his friends.

Unfortunately, he'd inherited little of Pippa's comeliness, taking instead after his father, whose gaunt and gangly puritanical figure came across as rather awkward. But apart from that, I have to say I found him a very personable young man with impeccable manners, and I recognised straight away how well Pippa had done in every respect and how much of her friendly manner had rubbed off on her son. And so I told her that she'd actually measured and shaped really well. Sanford, who hadn't been party to our conversation and didn't get the allusion, raised an ironic eyebrow at this, but this time I studiously ignored him.

'I thanked Marc for his friendly invitation; for his part, he seemed delighted that his parents had found someone congenial to hang out with, because he gathered that things were a bit awkward between his parents and Kelly's. Though everyone concerned never tired of emphasising that it was all down to Mary Ibbotson's dicky tum and, as Kelly confided in me later that evening, her father's limited ability to sweat. He was like a rodent, she said. Did you know', Preising interjected, 'that rodents can't perspire, or pigs for that matter, and that most predators can only sweat through the soles of the feet? Camels, though, have a phenomenal number of sweat glands, which really astonished me, as I'd always assumed they were like a sort of sack you filled with water, and that they were designed to lose as little of it as possible.'

No, I said, I hadn't known that, but now I did – and did these details on the perspiration rate of various mammals have any bearing whatsoever on his story?

No, Preising conceded, they didn't, but it was a truly remarkable and amazing fact all the same, and anyhow camels were something of a leitmotif in his tale.

And sure enough, another camel was soon to make an entrance. After the champagne reception at the pool, the group repaired as dusk fell to a small clearing in the palm grove. There, the picturesque ruins of an amphitheatre had been assembled from bits of rough-hewn stone and fragments of cement pillars, clearly modelled on the Roman amphitheatre at Carthage. It even had its own little stage, where folkloric events were occasionally laid on for the benefit of the guests. Powerful footlights cast a coloured glow up onto the trunks and crowns of the palm trees around the clearing. Meanwhile, a whole battery of spotlights, suspended above the stage on a transverse beam artfully disguised by plaster cladding, bathed the stage and the semi-circle where the audience sat in dappled coloured light. Throwing their flickering shadows onto the scene, several fire-bowls completed the illuminations, which a lighting technician from Tunis had been brought in specially to set up. However, he'd fallen out spectacularly with a celebrated Burmese florist from Antwerp, who tried to meddle with his colour palette, apparently because she felt the purple filter he was using clashed horribly with the delicate pink of her alstroemerias. Jenny, the German sports-car fanatic, who was the bride's best friend and had organised the whole ceremony, ushered the guests to their places, either on the stone steps or on lines of chairs with white linen covers. Ethereal drum and gong music from a CD called *Winds of the Desert*, which Jenny had borrowed from her personal Pilates trainer, played softly in the background.

Quicky was master of ceremonies. With his chest puffed out, he mounted the stage and paced up and down it a couple of times like a tiger before flinging his arms wide and formally bidding the assembled company welcome to the wedding of Kelly Ibbotson and Marc Rajani Greyling. He then called Marc up on stage, who to Preising's surprise had taken off his shoes and socks and stood in his dark suit looking somewhat forlorn between the plaster pillars. Jenny turned up the music. In the background, the tall silhouette of a camel emerged from the belt of palm trees. Kelly, also bare-footed, was sitting cross-legged on the back of the lavishly decorated animal and trying her best, despite its swaying and lurching, to maintain the appearance of a dignified and alluring bride.

The camel-driver was leading the beast by its reins. Jenny had made him swap his Rooney football shirt for a costume that she'd got an intern from the trading floor – who'd vainly hoped to get an invitation to the wedding in return – to copy from pictures of Tuareg horsemen in a travel brochure. She was pleased with the outcome; Kelly's white dress was set off wonderfully by the man's indigo-coloured robes, exactly the effect she'd intended. It also confirmed that she'd been right to pooh-pooh the intern's objections that there weren't actually any Tuareg in Tunisia.

But as he attempted to lead the camel up the two steps onto the stage, the fake desert warrior, his vision obscured by the unfamiliar headdress, stumbled and tripped over the over-long hem of his indigo-blue robes. This so alarmed the camel that it refused point-blank to go any further. Nor could it be persuaded to kneel down in the usual way to allow the bride to dismount with dignity. The camel-driver tried cajoling the beast, then resorted to tugging it ever more impatiently by the reins, as Quicky began kicking the backs of its knees. Kelly finally put an end to the unedifying spectacle by making a bold leap down from her high perch on the camel's hump into the arms of her waiting fiancé. Though totally unplanned, this wonderfully romantic moment prompted Kenneth Ibbotson to punch the air in triumph and shout out 'Bring her home, son!'

'Quicky then delivered a long speech, which I understood very little of. I wasn't surprised, frankly,' Preising said, 'because it was exactly like the presentations given by those management consultants that Prodanovic insists our firm uses, and which we pay a fortune for. I can't make head nor tail of them, either. Quicky went on about a merger and win-win situations, profits and bonuses, teamwork and investing in the future. He also sprinkled his address liberally with aggressive military metaphors and little gobbets of oriental wisdom. Courage and staying power, yin and yang, will power and humility, the force of flowing water and the wisdom of stones.

'Then the couple's closest friends read out messages of congratulation they'd written – with lots of mentions of health and happiness, but also of property ownership and key roles in Singapore – before incinerating them in the fire bowls. Quicky pronounced the happy couple man and wife, and they kissed. Rings were exchanged. Then came another ritual, where we all had to hold hands and form a circle round the bride and groom. You know how I hate all that stuff. In unison we wished them something or other, I can't remember what, but I do recall being between a young man with a gratingly loud voice and a diminutive Norwegian girl with tiny hands, who earned a packet speculating on fluctuations in grain prices. She left behind a delicate scent of marigolds and avocado on my fingers. The entire ceremony took quite a while and Mary Ibbotson, it seemed to me, looked relieved when we finally took our places for dinner.

'The chef, a young Carinthian maverick who'd trained in Tokyo and Sydney –' Preising started to tell me all about the wedding banquet, but I pulled him up short, as our stroll had given me an appetite and made me disinclined to listen to an exhaustive account of all the courses they'd consumed. Besides, I could all too easily imagine the kind of dishes a wild young Carinthian who'd learned his trade in Tokyo and Sydney would serve at the wedding of an English couple at a Tunisian desert resort where money was no object – or rather, where it was the be-all and end-all. Louisiana river crabs in a green tea jelly on a bed of date couscous; baklava with acacia honey, white truffles, pâté de fois gras and Tasmanian macadamias; or fillet of wagyu beef on sweet-potato rösti, and other such internationalised fripperies. Preising looked a bit taken aback at my interruption, but indulged me all the same to the best of his ability.

'Have it your way,' he said, 'I'll skip the dinner, then. Suffice it to say that it was, how shall I put it?... Well, wild is the best way to describe it, I suppose. Food from all around the world. Naturally only the finest of fare, truly exquisite stuff – no, don't worry, I won't go into detail – and beautifully served. Even so, I'm more into good old home cooking myself, in the best possible sense of the term, of course. Oh, and the wines, let me tell you... But no, I can see you'd rather not,' he shot me an inquiring look and checked himself.

'Anyhow,' he continued, 'I was seated at a round table at the far end of the dining room with five young people, none of whom were in the couple's closest circle of friends. I told myself I was perfectly happy to be on the periphery of things; after all, I was virtually a stranger, and my friendship with the bridegroom's family could scarcely be described as long-standing. Plus, it had the distinct advantage that we were the furthest away from the stage, where a musical combo was playing a sort of disco-friendly tango on electric instruments, making it easier for me to engage in sparkling conversation with my young neighbours. The disadvantage, though, was that I didn't have a ringside seat when, just before dessert – a pistachio semifreddo with caramelised bitter orange, served with a rich Sauternes – Pippa screwed up her courage and got up on stage. She rattled off the old chestnuts to such good effect that, by the time she'd read out the first two or three lines of the poem, a reverential silence had fallen over the assembled company. All around me, I could see people's faces rapt with concentration. Pippa acquitted herself magnificently. I could have listened to her for an eternity with my eyes closed; I was soon jolted out of my reverie, though, by the rapturous applause that greeted the end of her recital.'

The frantic clapping, however, had more of the character of a displacement activity, designed to dispel the embarrassed silence that Preising had misinterpreted as hushed reverence.

In fact, Pippa's performance had begun rather well. She'd been sitting at a table with Sanford, the Ibbotsons, the bride and groom, and their maid of honour Jenny and best man Rob – a young man who also worked in the financial sector, and who Marc had shared a flat with for several years before he and Kelly bought themselves a terraced house in Barnsbury for their thirtieth birthdays. Jenny, who was happy that the ceremony has passed off relatively smoothly, was regaling everyone with a long, involved story about the technical shortcomings of her new workplace, the head offices of a major bank, a new landmark building which was aiming to make an architectural statement in the City beside its rivals. The distinctive, unusual profile the architects had chosen to make the building stand out pushed the boundaries of what was possible in engineering terms, but it had also had the side-effect of creating distinctly unusual down-draughts. The upshot was that, in certain weather conditions, the revolving doors at the main entrance developed a life of their own and, overriding their electric servo motors, started spinning faster and faster. When an easterly wind was blowing and low pressure prevailed, the only way of entering or leaving the building was through emergency exits that gave onto a narrow, grubby alleyway. Ultimately, the revolving doors had to be replaced with automatic sliding ones. Even then, Jenny explained, there were still some days when you could only get out of the place during lulls between gusts of wind, with the result that, at lunchtime, the lobby would fill with great clusters of bank employees all waiting for an opportune moment to make a dash for it, a stampede that almost saw people trampled to death. On the other hand, spells of heavy rain could sometimes cause dirty water from the street to be blown like sea spray through the sliding doors as they opened, sweeping across the green-marbled lobby and spattering up against the monumental squeegee painting by Gerhard Richter that hung there. The Richter had already had to be extensively restored and protected behind a gigantic sheet of non-reflective glass. Everybody at the table seized gratefully upon this topic, which cut across all differences of class and age. Everyone had a story to tell about the dysfunctional nature of modern architecture, everyone that is except Mary Ibbotson, who'd never given it much thought. But even her husband began to thaw, telling people about the totally impractical urinals at his football team's new stadium.

It was in this laid-back frame of mind, self-confident, emboldened by a bit of alcohol, and with Preising's words of encouragement still ringing in her ears, that Pippa signalled the bandleader to pause the music as she mounted the stage. She stood in front of the microphone and calmly waited for the last conversations to die down before she began, with a steady voice and without glancing at the handwritten script in her left hand, to recite her poem. Straight away, she had the audience's full attention. Like puppies fixated on a juicy bone, like believers lapping up a preacher's words of wisdom, they gazed up at her. Pippa put it down to the power of the verse, being unaware that these young people were conditioned to hang on every word uttered by any confident speaker who had something to say: bank directors announcing profit targets, team leaders proclaiming the buzzword for the day, investment gurus with headsets dispensing recipes for success to the auditorium, professors explaining mathematical modelling, management consultants putting forward new strategies, and personal trainers spouting motivational mottos and offering tips on physical and spiritual fitness. It didn't matter to them who was speaking or what they were saying, it was all about the attitude of the person delivering the message. All that was required was self-confidence, presence and skill at vocal projection – a winning smile and smart clothes didn't go amiss either – and they were prepared to listen intently and applaud wildly. Even if they were being treated to a poem by an old Buddhist beatnik and deep ecologist.

But then Pippa lost control, letting her self-confidence slip for just the twinkling of an eye. It's hard to say what triggered it. Sanford, perhaps. Maybe it was one of those times when you suddenly catch sight of your faithful other half from an unfamiliar angle, and for a moment they look totally alien to you. You see their scrawny neck, their mobile Adam's apple, and suddenly you don't recognise yourself either. Just for a fraction of a second.

Instantly, a spasm of pained unease swept across the sea of upturned faces, a wave-like motion rippling through the room, palpable enough for Pippa to register it. It sent her into a downward spiral, which she would only finally pull out of two years later, when, standing at the top of the entrance steps to the English grammar school that was her new place of work, she looked down on the young student teacher leaning nonchalantly against her Prius, with his hands shoved in the pockets of his hooded top, and realised that she didn't need to take him as her lover but that she'd let him into her car and go off with him anyway. A downward spiral whose first coilings were accompanied by the rasping sound of the colour-filter wheel on the stage lights turning. Set in motion either by some electronic gremlin or by a well-meaning hotel employee, it changed the warm light that made her short grey hair shine and gave her cheeks a golden glow into a pale blue, which instantly extinguished any warmth. A downward spiral that gathered momentum as Pippa faltered and started to scan her notes, handwritten in royal-blue ink, for help. But the lines, penned in her regular, looping teacher's hand, refused to pull into focus, even when she held the paper at arm's length. A downward spiral that was already well underway by the time Kenneth Ibbotson dashed on stage to offer her the little pair of folding reading glasses he'd bought from a corner-shop chemist's in a Liverpool suburb; indeed, this only served to accelerate her decline. There Pippa stood, bathed in a cold blue light, stiff-hipped and grotesquely transformed into some old maid by Kenneth Ibbotson's drugstore reading glasses. She rattled off the old chestnuts with mounting desperation, but now the poem seemed interminable. A paralysing sense of horror gripped the assembled company.

If she'd been stark naked, with everything on show – her stretch marks, her saggy belly, her pubes flecked with the white hairs of old age – she couldn't have been more exposed than she was now, standing there shorn of all her self-confidence. The way her authority had suddenly evaporated was nothing short of obscene, and in the pale blue light she'd become a monstrosity who'd gatecrashed a celebration of self-confidence.

Pippa eventually made it to the end, line by line, word by tortuous word, before leaving the stage to thunderous applause, which hit her like the lashes of a whip. Lashes that she'd earned for having committed the cardinal sin of being unsure of herself and for exposing the wedding party to such a spectacle.

Preising would have been able to see all this perfectly clearly from his remote table if only he'd been willing to see what was plain to everyone else, rather than just seeing what he wanted to see. As it was, he enthusiastically joined in with what he later described as frenetic cheering.

His powers of observation weren't lacking in one respect, though. For he quite correctly identified that the remainder of the reception wasn't much different from other weddings he'd attended. There was a lot of chatting, drinking and dancing. And yet, it struck Preising, although this all passed off in a manner constantly verging on excess, it also seemed somehow very detached. People drank themselves into a stupor as though it was their duty, and went into the palm grove to throw up like they were executing some preordained plan. They also, Preising noted with some distaste, stuck their tongues in each other's mouths as though it was of no account. There was a feeling of excessive physicality and coolness in the way people danced, while their laughter was curt and ironic.

After a while, he hooked up with a group of men at the poolside bar, where Quicky, who was holding court, talked him into drinking shot after shot of a viscous, heavily chilled French vodka. Meanwhile, adopting Bronisław Malinowski's research method of 'participant observation', Sanford was pursuing his ethnographic studies by performing a kind of tribal dance with Jenny. Preising registered, more with amazement than out of any interest, how lithe she was, and how immaculately taut her figure seemed, like it was made out of some unknown, perfect material.

Before long, Pippa and the Ibbotsons called it a day. Preising tried to impress some of the young people by telling them Sanford's story about the Berber camel roast; after he'd finished, two of the girls took to addressing him as 'Mister Mungo Park'. The reference was lost on him. Then he got caught up in a conversation with Quicky. To stop himself from swaying about, the Englishman had flung his arm round the shoulders of a red-faced young man, who, smiling blissfully, appeared to take his role as a crutch as a mark of distinction. Preising noticed something strange and unfathomable about Quicky. For the most part, his delivery was halting and slurred, and Preising, who was pinned against a wall, found himself being coated with a light spray of his spittle. Yet names like Um Qasr, Nasiriyah, Rumaythah and Um Al Shuwayj tripped off his tongue as clear as a bell. He pronounced them like mystical terms. It turned out that they were all places where he'd served in Iraq. First as a member of an SAS squadron, part of the Coalition of the Willing in the 2003 invasion, and later – because, as he never tired of telling people, it paid 'way better' – as a contractor for a private security firm, an outfit he candidly described as a 'degenerate bunch of mercenaries'. Quicky recounted various war anecdotes, which Preising sincerely hoped weren't true, or at least were hugely exaggerated. And, if Quicky was to be believed, it was a short step from his role as a soldier of fortune to his job on the bank's trading floor – a post he'd taken up when, as he put it, he'd had enough of the 'fucking sand and the shitty ragheads'. 'Go on,' the florid-faced young man prompted Preising, 'ask him about his nickname. Ask him why we call him Quicky'. Preising did as he was bidden, and Quicky replied by lifting up his right hand to Preising's face and crooking his index finger as though he was pulling a trigger. 'That's why,' he slurred, 'quick trigger finger. That's why they were all so hot for me: the army, the firm and the bank.' He gave one of his braying laughs. In the background, the lithe Jenny went on dancing.

The wind was rustling the tops of the palm trees as Preising staggered back to his tent. Snatches of conversation and music kept drifting across as he lay on his bed, wearing only his underpants and socks. The seersucker suit lay in a crumpled heap on the Berber rug. Preising lifted his arm, took aim with an imaginary pistol at the point where the tent poles met, and crooked his forefinger. Then he laid his hand on his chest, where he could feel heartburn taking hold, and drifted off into a deep, dreamless sleep.

6

WHILE PREISING WAS SLEEPING, Britannia sank. In fact, the first signs of trouble were evident the evening before, but overnight things took another turn for the worse. The London interbank market had already ground to a standstill. While the capital was still shrouded in darkness, countries whose markets were trading desperately ditched their sterling reserves at a huge loss. A cabinet meeting called by the prime minister sat up all night in Downing Street until daybreak, watching as the pound sank to an all-time low, a fall in value that suddenly became a nosedive when, at 9 a.m. local time, the London Stock Exchange opened for business. Trading really ought to have been suspended that day, but as yet no consensus had emerged on who was to blame for this appalling mess, and until things became clearer the main priority was not to spook Britain's European and Transatlantic friends. This delay had disastrous consequences, though, as the computer programmes responsible – or rather not responsible – for most of the transactions proved ill-equipped to deal with a scenario that no-one up till now had even thought possible and so the system's feedback loops went haywire and within minutes had wiped billions off the value of shares before anyone could intervene. At 9.05 a.m. GMT, trading was finally suspended. At the same time, the Chancellor of the Exchequer was the first to go on record with what was already blindingly obvious, announcing that under these circumstances the country would no longer be able to service its horrendous sovereign debt. As he spoke, Marc and Kelly, for whom it was already five past ten, were fast asleep in their Bedouin tent. At precisely that moment, the bill for the wedding, which they were due to pay in Tunisian dinars, outstripped the value of their London terraced house in pounds sterling, with eighty percent of the house still owned by their bank – a bank whose lawyers were already declaring insolvency and drafting an e-mail to the employees advising them to bring a cardboard box into work that day.

By the time the prime minister met the press to announce that Britain had gone bankrupt, Saida had already been up and about for hours, getting the resort shipshape again with her team of bleary-eyed staff. They picked bottles and broken glasses out of the flower beds and shovelled vomit into a wheelbarrow, and Saida made Rachid go into the pool to fish out a recliner that had been thrown in and wake Kelly's brother, who was still bobbing about in his yellow rubber ring, with his head lolling back towards the water.

At the same time as European finance ministers were holding a somewhat panicky and chaotic teleconference, Saida finally found time to go and supervise preparations for the breakfast buffet, before withdrawing to her office with a cup of coffee and, as was her habit, catching up with the latest world news on the *Tribune de Genève* website. She always found herself hoping there'd be a mention in the section on local politics of the communist city council-lor she'd met during her time at hospitality management school, and who she still carried a torch for, though her infatuation was totally one-sided and unrequited.

On this particular day, though, she never got that far. After a brief moment of shock and a swift fact-check on the BBC and CNN websites, she picked up a pocket cal-culator, totted up the wedding costs, including bed and board for 72 guests, and arrived at a rough figure of six hundred thousand dinars, which amounted, at least a few hours ago, to about a quarter of a million pounds. She got on the phone and instructed the accountant in her father's office in Tunis to debit the newlyweds' credit cards to the absurd tune of one million, two hundred and fifty thou-sand pounds apiece. Of course, she knew full well that even the happy couple's shiny black credit cards wouldn't cover that amount, but she was hoping the issuer would at least let them max out. She then dashed to the kitchen to tell the chefs and waiters to cancel the breakfast buffet and clear everything they'd laid out except for a basket of flatbreads and a dish of hummus.

She wasn't at all surprised when the news came back from Tunis that both credit cards had already been blocked, nor did she have any joy when she tried the credit cards of other guests, who'd bought rounds of drinks on tabs at the bar and given their card numbers. As things now stood, it seemed all credit cards issued by British banks had been cancelled; indeed, as far as she knew the whole system of international payment transactions was on the verge of collapse.

Slim Malouch's secretary told Saida her father couldn't come to the phone, not even to speak to his daughter. Saida hung up, cursing that apartment in a middle-class, new-build development on the outskirts of Tunis, which she wasn't supposed to know about but where she suspected her father was right now. So that was that, then. For the next few hours, she'd be on her own. It was time to act.

Sanford was woken by the insistent ringing of a small bell. At first, he wasn't sure where he was, only registering dimly that his wife wasn't beside him. It took him quite a while to extricate his spindly legs from the tangled bedclothes; muttering to himself, he groped around for his dressing gown. Meanwhile, Saida stood outside the tent, her hand still holding the clapper of the brass bell which the staff used to announce their presence – one of the many disadvantages of accommodating the resort's guests under canvas was that you couldn't go along a line of tents knocking on doors – and listened intently for any signs of life. When she finally heard the Englishman stirring, she smoothed down the trousers of her suit and, as a precaution, tweaked her jacket hem to make sure it was sitting straight. She was now ready to face the bridegroom's father, the person she'd chosen to approach in this delicate situation, to let him know not only that the prime minister had just declared Britain bankrupt but also that, thanks to the pound's massive slump, his son had run up a hotel bill of such-and-such an amount. Here, she quoted a figure that struck Sanford as utterly fantastic, notwithstanding that he, like everyone else, had got used to hearing astronomical sums over the past three years. No doubt, settling up was going to be a very painful business, she added. Unfortunately, she went on, it was also her sad duty to inform him that all credit cards from British banks, presumably including his, had apparently been blocked, so could she ask him whether he or his son had a foreign currency account anywhere they could draw on? She hated to put it like this, but it could prove very useful in avoiding any unpleasantness.

Sanford, resplendent in an extra-bulky towelling bathrobe and slippers made of turquoise goatskin, immediately bridled inwardly at this. Somehow he'd always known it would come to this. Forewarned was forearmed. He'd always said this was what would happen, so he wasn't fazed. Even so, he was taken aback by the immediate implications, which Saida, albeit reluctantly yet still, now that her pecuniary interest could no longer be disguised behind a charming veil of hospitality, quite peremptorily spelt out to him.

She presented him with a stark choice: either the wedding guests pooled their resources and settled the bill forthwith, and in such a way that it could be verified – one option, say, would be to make a transfer in Swiss francs to the Malouf family's account in Geneva; in this case, she'd even be prepared to discuss a significant discount – or she'd have to ask the whole party to vacate the resort by two o'clock that afternoon at the latest. A simple breakfast had been laid out for them, she said, but other than that she was now duty-bound to ensure that no further expenses were incurred until such time as this whole unpleasant situation could be cleared up. Accordingly, all the resort's facilities – the spa, the tennis courts, the pool and of course all the restaurants and bars – were now off-limits, and she'd also be obliged if they'd keep their energy consumption and showering to an absolute minimum.

By now, it was beginning to dawn on Sanford that he was actually rather badly prepared for what lay ahead, and that the fact that he'd always said it would come to this would be a sublime irrelevance. Nonetheless, those were the exact words he greeted his wife with after tracking her down in her favourite bolt-hole, where she'd been sitting since dawn, sunk in abject misery. She'd been completely unable to concentrate on her book, which was quite unlike her, nor had the spectacular sunrise and the steadily rising temperature succeeded in lightening her mood. Pippa took the bad news on board resignedly and remarked that she'd seen it coming. She said she really wasn't sure if this would change the world in any significant way, or whether it would mean for instance that things like reading poetry aloud might become important again, and she refused to accompany her husband on his unenviable errand of going to tell the newlyweds that they were ruined and about to lose their jobs. She was adamant that, for the moment, her place was here, under the merciless heat of the African sun. She'd rather stay here, she needed to get her head around certain things, things that had nothing, absolutely nothing, to do with financial losses and stock market crashes. In other circumstances, perhaps, Sanford would have been surprised at her uncharacteristically pathetic tone, but for the present he had no choice but to trot off like some unshaven Mercury in trekking sandals and tell his son about an event whose full scope he still couldn't gauge himself.

'I was standing,' Preising recounted, 'just outside my tent, in my swimming trunks and with a towel under my arm, ready to do a few lengths of the pool before breakfast, when Sanford, who was clearly on his way to Marc and Kelly's bridal tent, bustled past me. "The pool's closed," he called out to me over his shoulder, "and don't shower for too long, either." He couldn't have known that Saida's new house rules, which I still knew nothing about myself at that juncture, didn't apply to me. At the time, then, I surmised that last night's revelries must have rendered the pool unusable, so I got dressed and went straight in to breakfast, where I immediately found myself in an extraordinarily awkward situation. For, quite counter to my expectations, when I walked into the dining room I wasn't confronted by the usual lavish breakfast buffet. In place of the baskets brimming with fruit, the jugs of freshly squeezed juice, the cold platters of French cheeses, roast beef and Spanish ham, the cake-stands with pâtisserie and the boards with baguettes wrapped in white napkins, the only things on the long serving table were a single basket of flatbreads, a dish of chick-pea dip and couple of thermos flasks of coffee. A lone waiter was busy clearing away the last of the china plates and silver cutlery; this task done, he proceeded to whisk the damask tablecloths off the Formica tables with a theatrical gesture. And yet, though she surely had more important things to attend to, it transpired that Saida had left specific instructions that a small table to one side of the dining room should be laid for me. It was almost groaning under the weight of food on it. But although,' Preising assured me, 'I had no inkling of what was happening in the wider world and how it had impacted on our little desert oasis, and so could make no sense whatsoever of this strange new arrangement, I still felt decidedly reluctant to sit down there, and I was just about to beat a discreet retreat when the waiter caught sight of me and, rushing over with his arms still laden with damask tablecloths, ushered me fulsomely to the place that had been set aside for me.

'Presently, Saida appeared, bringing me – along with the bad news – my *café au lait* and a sheaf of printouts from the online edition of *Le Figaro*. Rather alarmingly, the websites of *The Times* and the *Financial Times* had already gone down. I can't honestly say I was particularly surprised, I always knew that this would happen one day, maybe not with the speed it did, practically overnight, but all the same it had been obvious to me for ages that it was only a matter of time before something like this occurred.

'Saida told me she'd already arranged my transfer to the airport, as she was sure some far-reaching decisions now awaited my attention back in Switzerland. The only thing was that, for the time being, no-one could say when a suitable car would be available. Then she left me to get back to my breakfast, which, as you can imagine, I wasn't particularly enjoying.

'In the meantime, the dining room slowly began to fill with agitated young people. The devastating news had quickly done the rounds, but it was still sinking in. People read one another snippets of news from their smartphone screens, uttered anguished cries of disbelief, demanded that morning's papers and a proper Internet connection, and began arguing loudly with the staff about the meagre breakfast – not before, however, securing themselves a corner of flatbread and a scoop of hummus, since in private they'd already registered that times had changed. As soon as I could without appearing rude, I discreetly took my leave. Behind my back, two waiters forcibly prevented a graduate of Trinity College and hedge-fund manager from helping himself to the plate of cold meats I'd left. By now, I was fearful that some ugly scenes were in the offing.'

In effect, what Preising was presenting me with here was a variation on the by-now familiar theme of 'Where were you when Britain went bankrupt?'. Latterly, this genre had taken over from the earlier 'Where were you on 9/11?', a question that constantly forced you to recall the first time – hundreds more were to follow – when you looked at a TV screen and saw a plane crash into one of the Twin Towers. Likewise, we all now vividly remember the moment when the baby-faced PM in his baby-blue silk tie – an unduly optimistic and frivolous choice in the circumstances, I always thought – commenced his speech with the words 'In thirteen hundred and forty-five, when King Edward the Third told his Florentine bankers…' Sure, it had far less visual impact than 9/11, but it's still seared on our collective memory.

Incidentally, my two answers to the respective questions were: sitting in front of a portable TV in the boardroom of a haulage firm in Bayreuth, where all the staff had gathered to watch the tragedy unfold; and watching a flat-screen TV in the cafeteria at the University of Lucerne. In Preising's case, he'd been at home, in the kitchen, watching his housekeeper's television, when he'd seen the planes, and in his air-conditioned Bedouin tent when he'd heard the PM – here he picked up the thread of his story again – 'I'd retreated there to escape the febrile atmosphere in the breakfast room and to flip through the satellite channels to try and get an overview of the situation. Everywhere I looked there were agitated faces. Anchormen reading newsflashes, hastily made-up reporters, sweating experts. All the talk was of an impending financial meltdown, an epidemic. As you know, neither of those actually occurred to the catastrophic extent that was being predicted in all the TV studios and the special supplements produced by the world's newspapers that first morning.

'Pretty soon, I tired of all the jargon. The expert commentators were trying to outdo one another with their draconian measures for dealing with the crisis, each more drastic than the last, it seemed. Alternately, these seers forecast either a financial holocaust that would engulf the entire world, or a great cleansing catharsis. Meanwhile the politicians, according to their ideological standpoint, proclaimed the failure of capitalism, neoliberalism, ordoliberalism, the market economy per se, the financial markets, the welfare state, or even in some cases the whole democratic system. I finally settled on a news channel which I thought, in the midst of all this verbiage, had hit upon a compelling format with the apposite title '*No Comment*'. The programme consisted of nothing but a steady, long camera shot of a bustling crossroads in the City of London. The left side of the screen showed a greenish mirror-glazed skyscraper; this building appeared to be suffering the architectural equivalent of a tickly cough, inexplicably and convulsively disgorging large clusters of young people out onto the street at irregular intervals. Battling against strong gusts of wind, virtually stampeding one another and carrying cardboard boxes full of framed pictures, rowing trophies and potted plants, they lurched out into the rain, only to be confronted by an angry crowd who, gesticulating with raised umbrellas and home-made banners, vented their fury on this wretched human sputum, whom they clearly held responsible for the whole mess.'

Unusually exhausted by the previous evening's carousing, Preising nodded off again over this grotesque and decidedly surreal spectacle, and so was in no position to report on what happened next at the resort.

A crisis meeting was held in the dining room, at which Sanford soon found himself taking the natural role of leader. Because most of those present had, before going to work in the City, studied at the world's top universities, now that the curtain had fallen on their high-flying careers it was understandable that they should look back with fondness at the years they'd spent suckling at the bosom of their Alma Mater, and accordingly chose the person with the highest academic qualifications as their spokesman. Sanford seized this opportunity, turned the dining room into an impromptu lecture theatre and set out their options. These were basically the same as those Saida had presented him with, though Sanford took care to dress them up for his audience so as to make them less stark and brutal. Even so, no sooner had he finished than a storm of indignation broke out, and it was only his eloquently phrased appeal for peace and calm that prevented the mob from storming the kitchen, as a signal that they weren't prepared to be treated like this. Of course, it was also entirely possible that the raging hangovers most of them were suffering from may have had a bearing on their decision. Unfortunately, though, the downside of stopping a piece of direct action that would at least have generated a sense of community was that Sanford's calls for unity and solidarity at this difficult time fell on deaf ears. Instead, as the first texts terminating people's contracts began to arrive, the gathering fragmented into splinter groups, which came to terms with the collapse of their world in radically different ways.

Willy and Quicky, both of whom were acutely aware of social barriers, immediately realised that these barriers had now been torn down, and swiftly formed a fateful misalliance. They agreed that the situation called for some calm reflection, which in their case meant flaking out at the pool, downing a few beers, and maybe taking a dip in the cool water to shake off the effects of last night. Only when you'd cleared your head should you start worrying. Sanford's warning that Saida had been very clear about them not using the pool was blithely ignored, and a gang of thirty men joined Quicky and Willy. Indeed, Saida could do little to enforce her bathing ban. Rachid, armed with nothing but a net and flanked by his friendly greyhound bitch and her clumsy puppies, had express instructions to stop every-body but Preising from using the pool and the recliners, but wisely chose to avoid direct confrontation when faced with the advancing horde, and after a brief exchange of words across the length of the shimmering pool, in which Quicky deployed the barking Arabic he'd picked up in Um Qasr and Basra, withdrew to the adjoining palm grove, where he bombarded the group with unripe dates, all of which missed their mark.

In the meantime Saida, resolutely looking to the future, had started to try and contain the economic damage of the lean spell they were doubtless in for by paying off most of her staff and sending them back to live in their village at the far end of the oasis for an indefinite period. They should think about how they'd earned a living before the Malouch family arrived, she told them, and reassured them that good times would surely come again. But the willing servants in their brilliant white harem pants and oxblood-red waistcoats, who'd trotted off back home clutching their slim yellow final pay packets, were already being missed at the poolside bar by Willy, who kept calling angrily for a beer. When nobody came to take his order, he smashed the glass door of the locked drinks fridge behind the bar with a tennis racquet and made himself popular with his new friends by handing out chilled beers all round.

Almost in unison, a polyphonic cheeping, peeping and buzzing announced the next wave of sackings. This time, it was Quicky and most of the young men and women assembled round the pool who fell victim; most of those who'd followed him were the same people who congregated round him in the City, in the team of analysts and traders he headed up. Over the last few years, their risky and ruthless style of trading had made the bank hundreds of millions of pounds, and now that everything had gone belly-up they'd chalked up many times that sum in losses, too. While all this was happening, back at the offices in Gracechurch Street, a young woman in a navy-blue pinstriped skirt – that same intern who'd hoped in vain for an invitation to the wedding for sewing the Tuareg costume – was crawling around under the desks on the trading floor, disconnecting the terminals from the network, as she'd been asked to, and having her bottom ogled by bewildered men in expensive casual wear carrying cardboard boxes under their arms.

This round of dismissals were the last messages to reach the desert from England. Soon after, everyone's mobile went dead, as the Tunisian phone company concluded that sharing roaming tariffs with British mobile telecoms networks was too risky a business in the light of recent developments. This collapse of all lines of communication provoked the most diverse reactions from those who'd just become unemployed. Some people's eyes filled with tears, while others lapsed into helpless, hysterical laughter or an equally intemperate effing and blinding. A faint sudder ran between the narrow shoulder blades of a skinny brunette, which in other circumstances might have been construed as attractive but which in this case was triggered by the delusion that she'd been buried alive in sand out in the desert. Quicky, who had by now stripped off down to a pair of creased chinos and was sitting on a recliner with his legs splayed, reacted nonchalantly, taking his useless mobile phone and, with a deft flick of his wrist, skimming it into the dazzling blue pool. There, it accounted for the first bloodshed that day, as it didn't just sink like a stone when it hit the water but instead, thanks to its slim profile, skipped across the surface three or four times and hit a young woman swimming in the pool who ran a private London crèche – and who up to that point had borne a passing resemblance to Romy Schneider – square in the mouth, knocking out her front teeth.

Inspired by this collateral damage, Quicky rose from his recliner to make a speech, and at that precise moment Preising, refreshed and rested from his nap, reappeared at the poolside.

'Heaven knows, it was scene of utter confusion that met my eyes – and in that respect it followed on seamlessly from the London street scene I'd nodded off over, and which had haunted me in my dreams. The big difference was that here the sun was beating down mercilessly, and the midday heat was almost unbearable. The whole place was bathed in a mercury-silver light which made things stand out really sharply, picking out all the beautiful features, but also all the ugly ones, too, with absolute clarity and somehow lending them a kind of immobility that reminded me of the 'tableaux vivants' at the Oberammergau Passion Play. A young woman was sitting on the edge of the pool, crying; in spite of the blood-spattered hand towel she was pressing to her lips, I recognised her as someone who'd caught my eye a few days before because of her striking resemblance to Romy Schneider. Two girlfriends were comforting her, stroking her wet hair and trying to calm her down. Meanwhile, her fiancé, a floor trader from the British aristocracy, was diving in the pool to find her missing teeth; when he surfaced, strands of his thinning hair were plastered across his forehead.

'Quicky, who evidently didn't give a damn about the furious looks the woman's girlfriends were shooting him, launched into a long speech, the gist of which was that a new age was dawning and that he could tell them one thing for sure, and that was that a war was coming, no question, and if the shit hit the fan then people would have to join up and serve their country, if necessary in Her Majesty's forces but preferably with a private security firm. They needn't worry, he told them, he knew they were good guys and he'd happily go into battle alongside them, every man jack. If the situation demanded, then they'd swap the trading floor for the alleyways of Basra, the oilfields of Al-Qurna, the woods of Flanders or the streets of Berlin, for all he cared. Once a team, always a team! With this battle cry, he brought his speech to a close and raised his beer bottle in salutation. Several of his listeners did likewise, echoing his cry, though it seemed to me they did so more ironically, or at least I hoped that was the case.'

Jenny reacted to the changed circumstances in a far less belligerent way, but more single-mindedly for all that, when she decided to throw overboard her entire value system, which now seemed obsolete and no longer future-proof, and replace it with a new one grounded in the concepts of love and family. She confessed this new love of hers to a completely dumbfounded Sanford as she nestled, utterly exhausted, in his sweaty armpit after their first wild bout of lovemaking – which he'd found himself willingly engaged in after a brief wrestle with his conscience – and, twiddling her fingers in his sparse greying chest hairs, announced her intention of starting a family with him.

Jenny actually quite surprised herself at how attractive she suddenly found this haggard academic, who was around the same age as her father. After all, only a few hours before, his leering and his clumsy attempts at dancing had come across as laughable at best. How different he appeared now in the light of this new day; she noticed the natural authority with which he'd taken charge. What was more, he'd spent his whole life backing the right horse and not let himself be seduced from his settled intellectual realm by the lure of making a quick buck, something which in the event had turned out to be a will o' the wisp. A professorship at a university that had withstood the storms of history for five hundred years, a house with the mortgage all paid-off and a wife whom Jenny would be able to knock out of the picture with a single lithe swing of her hips. So she grasped this opportunity before someone else did and, taking Sanford by the hand, pulled him behind a palm tree, pinned him back against its rough trunk, unbuttoned his shirt, declared her passion for him, exploited his confusion and drove him to a peak of randiness by guiding his hands to her firm breasts. Though this last move seemed to belong to the value system she'd just left behind, she justified it to herself on the grounds that these were the hands of her future husband and father of her children. So it was that Jenny laid the foundations of her new future, after the old one had been ground to dust, not two hours before, between the millstones of the market.

The post-coital Sanford, his lust sated for now and in the process of regaining his analytical faculties, buried his nose in Jenny's hair, breathed in the subtle scent of her expensive shampoo, and weighed ridiculousness and litheness in the balance. Certainly, he was laying himself open to ridicule, he had no illusions on that score. In the circles he moved in, older men with girlfriends their daughters' age were considered absurd. Why, he was himself only too ready to condemn colleagues who got involved with female students as stupid old fools, though here he conceded to his credit that Jenny was well past student age. Then again, it surely had to count as the heights of stupidity for a man to fall in love with the bride's maid of honour at his son's wedding – and he was already quite sure that was what he'd done. Yes, by his own standards he was a ridiculous man. On the other side of the scales, though, was Jenny's litheness. The lithe Jenny. Her litheness weighed heavily, all the more so because events back home seemed to herald a new beginning – one, moreover, in which men like him, who had been on the side of the angels their whole lives and had spent their best years pondering how society should be organised, would be indispensable. Viewed in the correct light, therefore, he was entitled to this litheness; it was for the greater good, he told himself. For an instant, this thought seemed perfectly logical to him, then just as suddenly it was of no further consequence, as he settled for living with both ridicule and litheness.

'I turned away with horror from the scene at the pool and went off in search of Saida, who I eventually tracked down in her office behind reception. I asked her how things stood with my car to the airport, as I'd realised in the interim it would be a wise move to get away from here as soon as possible. Saida, whose dignified façade was growing notice-ably more mask-like, told me that a car had been ordered and that, as far as she knew, a driver was on his way here, but in all honesty she didn't have the faintest idea when he'd arrive. It seemed the situation had gone rapidly down-hill, and she was afraid that certain things had been set in motion in Tunis, perhaps throughout the country, whose immediate consequences she still couldn't gauge. She'd been trying for hours to get hold of her father, who was always incredibly well informed about even the slightest seismic tremors in Tunisian politics, but unfortunately she hadn't managed to reach him yet. She could of course offer me a seat on the coach she'd ordered to get rid of the English wedding party. However, the bus operator she nor-mally used was still feeling the effects of the accident with the camels, so she was trying to find a replacement before the group found out that British Airways and all the other UK carriers had been grounded at Tunis-Carthage Airport due to unpaid landing fees. She asked me to treat this piece of information with confidence, otherwise she feared she'd never get the Brits off her back. Casting my mind back to Quicky and his gang at the pool, I could appreciate her concern, yet on the other hand I thought it pretty callous of her to wash her hands of her unsuspecting guests and pack them off to the airport, where they'd find themselves marooned in perpetuity in the air-conditioned departure hall.

'My conversation with Saida was interrupted by Rachid, who came into the office holding a transistor radio to his ear and with his greyhound and pups in tow; he told Saida there'd been nothing but music on the air for the past two hours. I thought it might be a good idea at least to go and pack my bags. As I left the office, I caught sight of the Norwegian grain trader with the fragrant hands doughtily trundling a trolley suitcase, easily large enough to fit herself in, down the palm-lined avenue and disappearing through the stone archway into the desert. I was deeply disconcerted by this, and for a moment her determined stride made me think she'd actually decided to walk all the way to Tunis, dragging her case behind her. Because my curiosity was aroused, and because I hoped she might have organised herself some transport that I could cadge a lift in, I went after her, left the walled compound through the archway and gazed down the endless strip of black asphalt running across the desert. She was nowhere to be seen. Swallowed by the shimmering heat. Evaporated from the searingly hot tarmac. I was too late; she should never have been allowed to leave the resort. She was such a dainty little person. And a Norwegian to boot. Then again, I thought, getting a grip of myself, even tiny Norwegian wheat traders have some measure of resilience against the desert and don't simply vanish into thin air. Maybe I'd been mistaken, or seen a mirage. Or maybe I really was going out of my mind? I turned around, and there she was, sitting on her suitcase in the shadow of the wall and swinging her legs. I went up to her and, as is my wont, tried to strike up a conversation, assuming she could use cheering up, but it turned out she was perfectly content. They'd been told to clear their rooms by three that afternoon, leave the compound and wait for the buses to take them to the airport. She'd simply followed these instructions. There was no reason to start behaving in an uncivilised way, after all. For her, the most important thing now was to get back home as quickly as she could. I was just about to tell her that all flights to England had been suspended, but she preempted me by saying she wasn't going back to London but flying directly to Oslo. The crisis was a chance for her to make a fresh start; for a long time now, she'd had this dream of opening a bakery in Grünerløkka making cupcakes – little American cakes topped with coloured sugar icing, she explained.

'So you see,' said Preising, 'people were handling the situation in very different ways, and I started to wonder how my friend Pippa was coping, though I was sure that she was taking it all very calmly and sensibly. At that point I didn't know about Sanford's shameful betrayal.'

No, Preising genuinely had no idea of how the two reagents of ridiculousness and litheness had combined fatally and, with the ruthlessness of new lovers, sent the stumbling wife of the sociologist spinning down into the abyss after thirty-five years of marriage.

After another coupling with Jenny, where she gave

further proof of her litheness and its benefits, Sanford felt so much himself again, inwardly at least, that he was able to persuade her that it wouldn't be a good idea for them to both go and find his wife and explain about the new state of affairs. He needed to perform that difficult task alone, he told her. Jenny kept saying that she was wracked with guilt whenever she thought about their marriage and how it was now in ruins. She wanted to avoid at all costs any suspicion that she'd been the sower of discord – she purposefully used this literary turn of phrase, having intuited about three-quarters of an hour ago that an academic mode of expression was now at a premium, though she'd have been hard put to say where it came from. Sanford was able to swiftly put her mind at ease on that point. His marriage, he reassured her, had been on a knife-edge ever since the death of their daughter three years ago, and Jenny coming on the scene had just been the guillotine, as it were, that sliced through the last strands of skin holding together the head and the torso – metaphorically speaking, he added. In his and Pippa's case, a separation would simply confirm the statistical prediction that nine out of ten couples who suffer the loss of a child split up within eighteen months. Which all goes to show, the naked Jenny replied, that even love is subject to the power of statistics, like the sheep to the sheepdog, and the sheepdog to the shepherd. Did he see what she was driving at? Absolutely, said Sanford, causal chains, and kissed her on the forehead. That's it, Jenny answered contentedly, causal chains, as strong as the bonds between us. By now, Sanford's head was swimming, so to extricate himself from this semantic thicket, he pulled on his sand-coloured shorts over his bare bottom, slipped on his sandals and set off to end his marriage.

Walking straddle-legged, and enjoying the way his exhausted member dangled freely in his shorts, he climbed the steps up to the Terrace of the Beys, where he found his wife in exactly the same position he'd left her hours before, with her eyes shut and her face turned to the blazing African sun.

Pippa, though, only conveyed an unchanging impression to the kind of inattentive observer Sanford was at that moment. In fact, she was well on the way to contracting a serious case of sunstroke; what's more, she was enjoying every minute of it, so perfectly did the sensations that accompanied it – her cerebral cortex shrinking, a progressive dehydration, points of light dancing behind her closed eyelids and a mild sensation of giddiness – accord with her disoriented and confused mental state.

Their discussion didn't last long. Sanford took great exception to her scornful laughter.

'I found Pippa,' Preising recounted, 'sitting bolt upright on the far side of the Oriental couch. Her eyes were fixed on the horizon. She asked me to sit down next to her. Without knowing what had just happened, I asked her how she was. She attempted a smile, then her face dissolved into a flood of tears. With only the best of intentions, I reached for her hand, still thinking that she was upset about the state of the British economy. Pushing my hand away abruptly, she stood up, stumbled and lurched towards the sheer drop in front of the terrace. If that little carved side table hadn't been in the way, only some courageous intervention on my part could have saved her from plummeting into the tops of the palm trees. As it was, she ended up sprawled, half-sitting and half-lying, across the table. In response to my questioning, she admitted that, unable to sleep, she'd come up here at the crack of dawn and had been here ever since without drinking a drop of water or having a single bite to eat. I announced my intention of taking her to her tent straight away, but she indicated that she never wanted to set foot there again, and asked if she could have a lie-down in my tent instead. Naturally, I immediately complied with her request, taking her by the arm and leading her down to my luxurious quarters. There, after a few sips of water, she told me about Sanford's unconscionable and, we both agreed, utterly ridiculous behaviour, which had, of course, been incredibly hurtful to her as well. At her request, I laid a damp cloth on her feverish brow, and as I crept quietly out of the tent I noticed that she'd already drifted off to sleep.'

The noise of what sounded like a riot was drifting over from the pool, so Preising gave it a wide berth and headed for Saida's office to ask her for something to eat, which he planned to share with Pippa. But instead of Saida, the only person he encountered there was the lifeguard, sitting glued to the television, on which a man was reading out an announcement. Preising waited patiently until the man had finished, at which point Rachid treated him to a long explanation of how an unlikely alliance of renegade Muslim

Brothers and the Marxist-Leninist Fourteenth of January Front had taken the opportunity provided by the crisis of capitalism to launch a second wave of the Arab Spring. This time, though, they were determined to see it through to the end, to have a proper clear-out that would rid the country once and for all of the fat cats and the toadies and lickspittles of the old regime, who'd survived the last revolution unscathed – in fact, who'd found themselves even better off in a democratic Tunisia after dividing up the spoils of those who'd been toppled – and redistribute their wealth among its rightful owners, namely the Tunisian people. The days of the powerful and rich family clans were numbered. Preising, who correctly assumed that these fat cats included the Malouchs, signalled his alarm at this, fearing not only for Saida's safety but also his own; after all, he was here as a guest of the Malouch family. Rachid reassured him that all the talk was of seizing property, not killing people – after all, they weren't living in Ben Ali's Tunisia any more – but failed to allay Preising's concerns.

Eventually, Preising found Saida in the sandy yard behind the outbuildings, smoking, gesticulating and talking into her mobile. The camel from yesterday's wedding was resting in the shade of a palm tree. Saida made no effort to conceal her worry, but still played down the full gravity of the situation. She didn't tell Preising, for instance, that Slim Malouch wasn't, as she thought, at his lover's house but was already in custody, or that Interpol had issued an arrest warrant for her brother, who as luck would have it was on a work experience placement with a hill farmer in the Vosges, something even their father didn't know about, or that the bailiffs must already be on their way to the *Thousand and One Nights Resort*. She did reassure him, though, that her car and driver would be here any time now. Preising wanted to know whether it wouldn't be wiser just to take any old car and drive to Tunis as fast as possible. Unfortunately, it turned out that the Carinthian chef had already taken off in the last available vehicle, and had also forgotten to leave the keys to the larder and cold store, so all that Saida was able to give Preising was a load of little bags of honey-roast peanuts and crisps to take back to Pippa.

Yet this diet of saturated fats, carbohydrates and electrolytes proved to be just what the English teacher needed to get back on an even keel. As Preising fastidiously packed his suitcase, she tore open bag after bag and tipped the contents into her mouth, washing it all down with great gulps of lemon water from the jug on his bedside table, perking up visibly and growing ever more animated as she did so. Certainly, the manic state she worked herself into was far better for her than the one she'd been in before, on the verge of dehydration and heat exhaustion, but what she gained in health she lacked in decorum. She began to make fun, in a way that Preising found shocking if wholly understandable in the circumstances, of her husband's absurd behaviour. It was unworthy of her, too easy a target for a clever woman like Pippa, especially when she started to direct her sharp-tongued insults at the former floor trader and her German sports cars. Preising would much rather have had his silent, dignified Pippa back at that moment. Serene, sovereign and standing above it all, he reflected as he wistfully consigned the leaky bottle of rose water to the wastepaper basket. That was just the way this Preising fellow was. Pippa, on the other hand, tormented as she was by the most conflicting of emotions, humiliated, hurt and seething with jealous rage and cold hatred, now started riffing on how young her rival was, knowing full well that, in this matter, biological imperatives precluded any possibility of a level playing-field from the very outset. She then put Preising on the spot by asking him whether he'd ever noticed how lithe Jenny was. He nodded silently in assent, though her question had been rhetorical and she couldn't have cared less about his response. In actual fact, she went on, she wasn't in the least bit jealous of Jenny, frankly she was welcome to a lifetime of arguing with the old smart-arsed dickhead; no, truth be told, it was Sanford she was jealous of, she envied him Jenny's litheness. I really wish — she exclaimed in fury, pummelling her clenched fists into Preising's soft duck-down pillow — I really wish I had a dick so I could shag her, the lithe Jenny. Hearing this, Preising, his brow damp with sweat and inwardly cursing his vivid imagination, fought desperately to stop a welter of lurid images from flooding into his mind. In this state, he found himself powerless to fend off the Englishwoman when she abruptly wrapped her legs around him and grasped him firmly by the back of the neck and pulled him down to kiss her. Things would doubtless have taken their natural course, which in all likelihood would have done neither of them any good in their current state of confusion, if they hadn't suddenly been startled by the blood-curdling scream of a camel in its death throes.

At this point, Preising interrupted our stroll again. I walked on a few paces to try and encourage him to keep moving, but he refused to budge, just standing there with his hands on his hips. 'It just wouldn't have been right,' he ruminated, 'it wasn't me who Pippa wanted. She was dreaming of having a phallus and penetrating Jenny.' Having announced this as though he was clarifying some abstruse point, he resumed his walk along the yellow perimeter wall, and I tagged along beside him.

The hubbub that Preising had avoided when he went looking for something to eat came from the group that had gathered around Quicky and Willy, and was chiefly due to the fact that the beer supplies were slowly running out. Also, the unsatisfactory food situation – nobody had had anything to eat since the bits of flatbread at breakfast – was gradually taking its toll on the general mood. The existential angst everyone was feeling, but which nobody wanted to articulate for fear of disappointing Quicky, finally manifested itself in an upsurge of discontent. As an experienced leader, Quicky saw straight away that action was called for, so under his command a raiding party set off for the kitchen wing. As they made their way there, the whole place seemed deserted, with not one of the willing servants who'd discreetly populated the resort up until yesterday now in evidence. What they did run into, though, was a group of lost souls, the bride and groom among them, who, dragging their suitcases behind them, were following Saida's instruction to leave their rooms and were on their way to join their tiny Norwegian friend, who was still sitting outside the gates lost in reverie, dreaming of a display cabinet full of colourful cakes. There was a brief exchange of words between the two groups but no voices were raised; they'd already grown so far apart that they didn't have much to say to one another. Like two different tribes, each engaged in its own ritual, they parted and went their separate ways.

Quicky's motley crew gained access to the kitchen easily enough but were thwarted by the massive steel doors of the cold store, despite their best efforts at bashing them open with a heavy-duty meat mallet. If no food was to be had there, Quicky decided on the spur of the moment, then they'd have to hunt some down, and began arming his troops with an assortment of sharp blades from a large knife block. That was the point at which Willy suddenly thought of his wife and children and discreetly melted away.

In the ensuing hours, two equally chance and trivial occurrences combined to trigger a series of events that culminated in an apocalypse of blood and flames.

The first concerned the camel owner – the fake Tuareg and Rooney fan. After the wedding, the plan had been for him to tether his camel to a palm in the courtyard behind the admin block and go to sleep beside it on a rush mat he'd brought with him, before making his way home the next morning at first light, with his paltry earnings for supplying the camel and for his performance in his pocket. But while the guests were at dinner, he'd seized the chance to filch a whole plate of the tempura prawns with harissa mayonnaise, which he'd found untouched at the poolside bar. He was hoping to present them to Rachid, and in return to be invited to share a hashish pipe with the lifeguard. He couldn't have known that, when Rachid moved to the desert, he'd renounced not only swimming but everything to do with the sea, including seafood. And so he'd had no choice but to eat the entire plate of this unfamiliar fare – which at first had conjured up images of a wide world he knew nothing about – all by himself. During the night the poor fellow, unused to such a protein-rich diet and doubled up in pain on his mat, thought he must be dying and threw up time and time again beside his camel, which gratefully accepted his offering, licking it up off the sand with its agile tongue. As dawn broke, Rachid took pity on the exhausted camel driver and gave him his own bed, where he slept through England's financial crash and remained for the whole of the next day, tossing and turning in a high fever, while his camel waited patiently for him out in the yard.

The second had to do with a conceited sociologist, who was irritated when a listener's attention wandered from his lectures, and a Swiss businessman, sitting together at a metal table in a Tunisian village square drinking sweet tea, and the businessman, who was wearing a pair of stained trousers, getting distracted by the sight of a fat policeman smoking a *boussetta* at the window of the gendarmerie opposite and piquing the Englishman into wheeling out the big guns and telling him the story of the stuffed and roasted camel, which Preising quite correctly identified as a shaggy-dog story so didn't take it at face value, though ultimately this became irrelevant when, that same evening, in the company of a group of drunken young people, he presented it as gospel truth to try and impress them.

It didn't take long for Quicky's knife-wielding, food-hunting band to stumble upon the camel in the courtyard. The moment he set eyes on it, Quicky, who had a sharp mind but a very poor knowledge of literature, and who'd only half-listened to Preising's story the night before, was able to reel off the entire recipe for roasted camel verbatim, entrancing his audience with the prospect of an authentic Tunisian feast. The gently protesting animal was promptly untied and led by its halter over to the swimming pool. Quicky peremptorily brushed aside objections from some in the group that there was no mutton, goat or quails to hand by remarking that extraordinary times called for improvisation, and that they'd find something to stuff the camel with presently. Rachid, alerted by the camel's terrified bleating and accompanied by his greyhound bitch and her four friendly puppies, appeared by the pool at precisely the wrong moment. It was also a very bad move for him, in a vain attempt to save his pets, to confront an angry mob of people, who found themselves stranded in a foreign country and facing the ruin of their very existence. In actual fact, Quicky had just been joking when, naked but for his rolled-up trousers and theatrically juggling a knife in his hands, he sashayed menacingly up to the lifeguard; after all, he didn't eat dogs. Rachid, meanwhile, squared up to his assailant with his fists raised, ready to protect his animals. But the blond young man, who the previous night had performed the role of crutch for Quicky with all the devotion of a junior fraternity member, crept up on Rachid from behind and smashed him over the head with the same tennis racquet that Willy had used to break into the drinks cabinet. The blow, which was delivered with quite some force, felled the former swimming champion like a palm sapling and pitched him face-down into the pool. As his powerful lungs filled with water, he thought he could hear the bell tolling on the yellow buoy off Sfax.

Blood had now been spilt in earnest; as a huge roar of victory greeted the lifeguard's drowning, Quicky realised that things had got completely out of hand. But he also saw that there was no way back from this madness. Taking hold of the camel by the halter and forcing it to the ground with violent tugs and kicks to its knees, he knelt heavily on the screaming best's neck and, to the jubilant roar of his former bank colleagues, thrust the long blade of the kitchen knife straight into its heart with all his might, as the camel stared at him with wide, uncomprehending eyes.

The dying animal uttered a long drawn-out guttural scream. Carried by the wind through the palm grove, it reached the line of tents and shocked Preising and Pippa out of their feverish tussle on the bed.

'So there we stood, facing one another in my tent with our hearts missing a beat and a spilt water jug between us. We knew instinctively that what we'd just heard was an animal dying. I argued that we should stay put, but Pippa wanted to find out what had happened. Reluctantly, I followed her as she took me by the hand and led me towards the swimming pool, from where we could hear wild screams and agitated shouting. Crouching down behind a low wall and clinging on to each other as if we were drowning, we were witness to a scene unrivalled in its crazed ferocity since the Maenads went on the rampage on Mount Cithaeron. The revellers had used their combined muscle power to haul the dead camel up by its hind legs and hang it over the gallows-like support for a large sunshade. There, they'd sliced open its belly, causing its innards to spill out over the glazed patio tiles. A slim brunette in skimpy shorts and a bikini was delving up to her elbows into the beast's entrails, while others were attempting to tear the felted hide off the cadaver. With a single well-aimed thrust, Quicky silenced the greyhound bitch, which was standing on the edge of the pool barking frantically at her master's lifeless body floating there. Then he picked up the whimpering puppies, one by one, and calmly slit their throats. As if petrified by this ghastly spectacle, we remained rooted to the spot, incapable either of intervening or – a far more sensible course of action – of fleeing. So, we stayed there behind the wall and watched as one group of maniacs lit a huge bonfire on the sand under the palm trees, using broken-up sun loungers for fuel, while others set about disembowelling the dogs. When they'd finished, in a gesture unparalleled in its sheer insanity, they stuffed the puppies back inside the slim body of their mother and then took the dead dog, her belly swollen with her butchered offspring, and shoved it into the bloody cavity they'd made in the camel. The loungers were well ablaze as they started dragging the camel over to the fire. But they never got that far; the fire set the dry bast at the base of a palm tree alight, and within seconds flames had shot up the long, slender trunk and ignited the fronds, turning the whole tree into a blazing, crackling torch against the gathering gloom of sunset.'

As the fire, fanned by the warm west wind, flashed over to the surrounding trees and the mob scattered under a shower of red-hot palm fronds, Pippa and Preising also took to their heels, only to be stopped in their tracks by the raging inferno as they tried to make it to the exit. Peering through the smoke and flames for a way out, they soon lost sight of one another in the thick haze. The burning palm grove was filled with Englishmen rushing around in a state of panic and yelling. Above their heads, in the intense heat of the fire, palm kernels were exploding like pistol shots. The tents flared up and fell like shot birds onto the expensive furnishings. Taking a wide arc, Preising ran towards the main building, calling out Pippa's name. Behind him, half the oasis now stood in flames. All of a sudden, like a ray of salvation, the bright beam of powerful headlights pierced the dense smoke. He heard someone calling his name, then Saida was by his side, steering him towards the leather back seat of a 4×4, which her driver had evidently brought through the rear entrance, just in the nick of time. Coughing, half-suffocated, blinded by the acrid smoke and with singed hair and glowing fragments of palm frond on his collar, he felt the powerful 4×4 surge forward. Ahead of them, burning tree trunks blocked their path. The driver slammed the vehicle into reverse, swung round the building, roared across the flowerbeds onto the curving entrance drive and rounded the ornamental fountain with smoking tyres. Ignoring some desperate guests who made a grab for the door handles, he turned down the central avenue, now lined with blazing palms, overtaking several people fleeing the compound, who had to fling themselves aside to avoid being run over, and bursting open their abandoned suitcases as he bounced over them, and finally made it out of the burning resort through the stone archway. There, dragging their trolley cases behind them, a long caravan of English tourists could be seen walking down the dead-straight road across the desert like latter-day Israelites leaving Egypt. They cast flickering shadows on the glowing red sand as they passed. Safely cocooned in the 4×4, Preising swept past them, his soot-smudged face pressed to the window as he tried in vain in the bright light of the fire to spot his companion's face among the fleeing hordes. For a long time, he kept looking back through the rear window at the inferno, which cast its flickering glow across the desert floor and stained the sky blood-red.

7

SAIDA'S CHAUFFEUR STEERED the black 4×4 through the bright moonlit night with its headlights extinguished. The black strip of asphalt showed up clearly against the light sand. At some point, he turned off the tarmac road and they continued on a dirt track, now with the lights switched back on. Now and then, the headlights caught a startled animal in their beam, standing stock still with reflecting eyes; to Preising, it seemed as though they were staring through him into the very core of his being, on which the bloody scenes he'd just witnessed were now indelibly seared. Then the animals kicked their hind legs and were off, disappearing into the dark desert and leaving him alone with his two silent companions. Almost imperceptibly, the terrain changed, as the sandy and stony wasteland gave way to an ancient rocky landscape. The road became steep and winding. In their mobile womb of toughened safety glass, cream-coloured alcantara upholstery and polished burl-wood trims, they crossed a bleak high plateau under a perfect starry sky. By now he had lost all sense of time. Dense vegetation replaced the barren desert.

'I remember us finally stopping at some isolated farmstead. There was an olive grower, still woozy from sleep, standing next to the 4×4 and staring in disbelief at the car keys Saida's driver had just thrust into his hand. We resumed our journey in a beaten-up old Peugeot. The cool night air whistled through the leaky windows, dispelling some of the sour smell of spilt goat's milk that pervaded the car. As dawn broke, the outskirts of Tunis came into view. Saida covered her head with a plain shawl. In an industrial estate, the driver pulled up beside a wire fence. A young man instantly appeared like he'd been expecting us and opened the locked gate. In the grey light of the new day, I stepped out of the Peugeot in front of a low corrugated-iron shed and started to stretch my stiff limbs but I was unceremoniously bundled inside the windowless building.'

It's hard to say what Preising must have been feeling as he was ushered into the neon-lit shed. Or to imagine how much he comprehended, or wanted to comprehend, about what he saw there. The narrow, hunched backs of children bent over long tables. For a moment, the air of hushed concentration and the total absence of children's voices made him think he was in some educational establishment. The dark little hands with pink palms expertly fitting electronic circuit boards, connectors and switches into small plastic casings. The gaunt, lanky youth with the dark features of a Southern Sudanese Dinka, who with blood-encrusted fingernails was peeling hard little stickers off a laminated sheet and placing them precisely in the corner of small plastic boxes. Preising thought he caught sight of the red *Prixxing* logo, and below it the slogan *Genius of Swiss Engineering*, which Prodanovic was so proud of and which Preising had paid an ad agency in Zurich a small fortune to come up with. Moncef Daghfous' voice resounded in his head.

Dab-handed little chaps. Dab-handed little chaps. Then there was the smoke-filled office with the little man lounging in a garden chair, who didn't even bother to take his shabbily slippered feet off the desk when Saida walked in. The television set in the corner, showing ordinary Tunisian people sauntering through a luxuriously furnished villa. A villa just like the one where, not four days ago – could it really be that short a time, it seemed like an age to him? – Preising had been a guest. The dirty glass filled with strong tea, which he gratefully accepted. Saida took off her shawl, crashed out on a mock-leather sofa between piles of old newspaper and greasy food wrappers, and fell into a deep sleep.

'"Are you angry?", the little man asked me', Preising said. 'Was I angry? No, that didn't describe how I felt, rather I was disgusted, and I thought of that young entrepreneur who, over a meal of *Zürcher Geschnetzeltes mit Rösti*, had been at pains to tell me that, when viewed with a measure of healthy detachment, the question of child labour wasn't as simple as it might appear. But from close up, certainly, it seemed perfectly simple. Simple and disgusting. But it turned out that wasn't what the little man meant, as I realised when he came right out and told me that, if he was in my shoes, he'd be hopping mad – after all, I was paying Malouch the going rate for properly qualified adult workers, whereas – as I could see with my own eyes – my precious products were actually being assembled by little Black Africans. "Monsieur Malouch takes a tidy cut for himself there, I can tell you," he said. Malouch, he assured me, had been taking me to the cleaners for over a year now, ever since he'd acquired this assembly plant, which could turn out goods at an unbeatably low cost and which was incredibly well-run – here he gestured with a nicotine-stained thumb towards his pot belly – from the surviving dependants of a former business rival at a scandalously knock-down price. Malouch's deceased competitor, he explained, had been an incredibly brave man, who'd gone to tackle a blaze in a phosphate plant armed with nothing but a shovel and a bucket of sand and lost his head in the process. In any event, he said, he had a very interesting proposition to put to me. anyway, the Malouch family's business empire was over and done with now, but since this operation probably didn't appear anywhere on the books and so could escape the outrageous nationalisation programme, he said he'd be prepared to keep managing the factory at his own risk; of course, in his new capacity as owner, he'd be in a position to meet me halfway on negotiating a new rate. In my situation, I thought it wisest not to respond to this utterly disgraceful and criminal proposal, so I signalled my disdain by maintaining a contemptuous silence.'

A silence which in actual fact might be more accurately described as a state of stunned speechlessness on Preising's part. However, Slim Malouch's renegade employee read it quite differently and wrongly, taking Preising, in spite or maybe precisely because of his down-at-heel appearance – he hadn't shaved for 24 hours and this, combined with his scorched clothes and tousled hair, made him look a bit of a bruiser – to be a real hard case. So, to prove that he was just as tough a nut, the man pulled out a mobile from the pocket of his grey gabardine jacket and called the security services to tell them he was holding Slim Malouch's daughter in custody.

Four uniformed officers came to fetch Saida. Grabbing her by the hair, they dragged her past the long work benches, as the children kept their heads down and went on with their work. The little man got up to stretch his legs, put his arm round Preising's shoulders and escorted him out of the building, pointing out as he did so how clean everything in the plant was. Outside, a young policeman opened the door of a patrol car. As Preising stooped to get in, he felt the manager's hand press down lightly on his hair, carefully guiding him in to stop him bumping his head on the door frame. 'Just give me a call,' he said in parting, 'and we'll discuss the new rate.' Then he shut the door behind him and waved at the car as it sped off. Preising looked back over his shoulder. He saw Saida stumble and fall, and then the policemen were kicking her as she lay on the ground and dragging her across the tarmac by the collar of her René Lezard trouser suit, with her blouse torn and riding up to reveal her pale stomach and the blue bra she was wearing. He felt like he'd witnessed this scene before somewhere, in a different context, under quite different auspices, but he couldn't put his finger on it. This inexplicable sense of dreamlike déjà vu was so enduring that, when the police dropped Preising off a quarter of an hour later in front of the Swiss Embassy, he wasn't sure whether everything he'd gone through over the past few days had actually happened.

Preising concluded his story by telling me about his return flight on a crowded tourist plane and being met by his housekeeper, who'd driven to the airport to pick him up. For one final time, he stopped on the gravel path. 'When I saw her face at arrivals,' he said, raising his hands as though it was in front of him now and he was caressing it tenderly, 'it struck me as the most beautiful I could imagine – and you know what my housekeeper looks like, right?' Indeed I did, as she came to visit him here regularly. Then he turned onto the path leading to the main block. 'Come on,' he said, 'Supper should be ready.'

So, what had been the point of all this – this sad story full of tragic coincidences? It was a tale with no didactic purpose to it.

Preising seemed deeply downcast by his own story. His face positively oozed unhappiness, with its sad, drooping nose, dry, cracked lips and watery eyes. But I couldn't take that into consideration now. 'So what was the point of your story, then?' I pressed him, mercilessly. Preising's response seemed pregnant with some secret knowledge on his part, yet also a deep anxiety about what he knew. 'Once again, you're asking the wrong question,' he said.